$\mathcal{A}$

$\mathcal{VICTORIAN}$

$\mathcal{MISS}$

$\mathcal{A}$ Kind of Courage

JANET
GOLDFINCH

To Marjorie
With all best wishes
Janet Goldfield

DEDICATION

To Eliza; and to all those countless
generations who, against long odds, managed
to survive.

CONTENTS

ACKNOWLEDGMENTS

The story owes its origin to a handed-down family tale. It was so intriguing that I decided to work on the clues available to erect a framework, and to reconstruct the historical background.

The factual framework was built using censuses, parish records, civil registration records and the certificates supplied. Access to these was provided largely by *ancestry.co.uk* and *findmypast.co.uk*. The *General Registry Office, genuki.org.uk* and *familysearch.org.uk* also played their part.

For the background I owe thanks to a multitude of sources: histories of the Victorian era, histories of costume, of food, of cotton manufacture, of places. Old maps and new helped me find my way through the streets of Birmingham, Manchester and Spondon. Contemporary newspapers contributed background colour in the guise of criminal cases, advertisements, weather; all accessed through the newspaper collection at *findmypast.co.uk*. My childhood memories of Spondon, garnered when visiting grandparents, were fleshed out by *spondononline.org.uk* and *spondonhistory.org.uk*.

The celebrity mentioned in the last chapter came as an improbable, though interesting, surprise. I knew nothing of this until I researched Eliza's later life and was most kindly given copies of newspaper cuttings and letters by the son of the subsequent Rector of Seagrave.

1
1880
SINK OR SWIM

The girl had huddled herself into the corner of a flight of steps as it turned down into the basement below. She sat close against the rough brick wall at her back, head bowed low, her skirt wrapped in tight folds about her legs for warmth, her arms crossed in front of her, clutching her shawl about her shoulders, the shawl he had flung out after her into the street. She tried to make herself as small as possible.

When she had found this place, she had been hidden in darkness, but it was early July and for the last hour or two it had been lightening, though still gloomy under heavy cloud. It was also raining, gently but steadily and, tucked in though she was, the wetness was seeping into her clothes.

A lamp flared in the basement and through the glass she could see a figure moving. If the occupant of the basement looked out, she would be seen. And what then? She would be driven away. Where could she go? Panic flooded her brain. There *was* nowhere to go. A tide of loneliness, abandonment, swept over her, engulfed her.

An impulse to escape made her half rise, stiffly. Her bruises were still painful, though there seemed nothing too bad to mend. She would go … But then the hopelessness of it all hit her anew. Where could she go? She might walk a little, look for other shelter. But what would she find, in this wasteland of houses and streets, all brick, all peopled? At best a half-built house. Even those were likely to be inhabited by outcasts she would shrink from. She curled herself again, back into a tight ball.

She must be careful too. Last night, and it had not been for the first time, she had been accosted, a drunken, filthy fellow; and she had run, he lurching behind. She had been faster than he and had left him shaking a fist, shouting curses. If she moved, she must try to look like a respectable servant, out early on an errand. To fetch a doctor perhaps. But such a ploy could serve her only for a while. What could she eat, what could she do, all the long day? And for all the long days more, for ever and ever. Fear grew.

She might catch cold: she surely would catch cold in this misery of wetness. And the cold would turn to worse and she would die. If only she were dead now, and it was all over. Girls like her drowned themselves, did they not? But she knew of no river here. The canal perhaps, but it was far away; and, in spite of a wish for oblivion, she shrank at the thought of its black, putrid waters.

The workhouse then. But that was a place of

dread: a great-aunt was said to have had a child that died there, an aunt in her own scandalous position. Terrible tales were told of the workhouse: it was a place of scorn, of hunger, of casual cruelty, a place to which you must never sink, never have cause to go. And they dressed them in a horrid yellow, girls like her, so that everyone would know.

Tears filled her eyes, tears of terror and self-pity and bitter self-reproach. She had wept a great deal since she had discovered her predicament. And two days ago she had wept again, when he had discovered it too. His fury had astounded her, shocked her to her very bones. He, her one thread of hope, had snapped it short.

The slight figure within the basement was joined by another, taller and more robust. The first, she surmised, would have been the kitchen-maid, come to stir up the fire; and the new and lumpier arrival the cook, using a cook's privilege of a few extra minutes of sleep.

She dozed a little in spite of herself. A noise startled her: the flinging-up of a sash.

'You. You there. Go away.' The bellow startled her. Arms made fierce threatening movements. A head and shoulders appeared in the gape of the window.

"Ow dare 'ee? Trash. Whore. Get away wi' thee. We dunna want no beggar-women 'ere. This 'ere bin a respectable 'ouse.'

She scrambled to her feet, aching with the movement of stiffened limbs; and began to run. Any way, any direction, anywhere to leave the contempt and the noise and the anger behind.

A figure turned its head to gaze as she scurried

wildly across a road. A new wave of panic and then her mind cleared a little. This wouldn't do: she was attracting attention. She must pretend that she was here, walking through the streets so early, to some purpose. She slowed her steps. She had not even a basket on her arm to lend her some credence.

A brewer's dray rumbled past, the horses which pulled it huge, their manes plaited, brasses jingling. There were carts: milkmen, bakers, calling their wares. She could smell the bread, being sharply reminded that she had eaten nothing but scavenged scraps since early evening two days ago. It was after that meal that she, hoping her father would be in a genial frame of mind with food inside him and a glass of beer beside him, had ventured to hint at her secret. She thrust the ensuing scene from her mind.

Minutes passed; hours passed. Her bladder ached; and she was occupied for a while finding a tunnel between the close-packed houses which took her through into a dismal court where washing drooped greyly from windows and flies buzzed round a couple of stinking privies.

She scurried back to the street full of distaste, wandering everywhere and nowhere, sitting where she could from weakness. No plan would come to mind. She pushed her hand into the slit between the waistband and skirt of her dress, hoping against hope. But the pocket held no coins, as she already well knew. There were only a pair of scissors, a needle-case, a handkerchief and a button-hook. Could she sell the handkerchief? It was embroidered, rather prettily, she thought wryly, by herself. Any money she might get for a handkerchief would not satisfy hunger for even an hour or two. Should she beg? The idea repelled her.

Then what could she do? Her mind screamed with the despair of it. She knew no-one in Birmingham, certainly not well enough to look to for help. The town was certainly the place of her birth, but they had left for Wolverhampton over half her lifetime ago when she was ten, in yet another move. They seemed to have been always moving, from one street to another, one town to another. Manchester was the place she knew best, where she had spent the last dozen years, moving from one street to another even there.

John Kirby liked to be near his work, he said. She had come to suspect that her father had another reason for movement, that he fled from tragedy, as if a place that had hurt him once would hurt again if he stayed there and that a new one would give him better fortune. That had proved a forlorn hope.

A street pump caught her eye. She cupped her hands and drank, disdaining the chained metal cup, relishing the cool wetness.

They had not been back in Birmingham long, told to pack up and leave Manchester almost as soon as the wedding was over, the whole lot of them. To cover the shame, she thought, the shame of everyone they knew scorning them, talking behind their backs, relishing the knowledge that her sister had no longer been a maiden when she married, was 'no better than she should be', that the stuck-up Kirbys were after all no better than the rest. Another tragedy, another hurt to flee from.

Oh, the scenes there had been early last year in

Manchester when their father had suspected, and the rage that had terrified her sister and the lover into February wedlock. Sarah-Ann had been desperate for marriage anyway, marriage that would save her reputation and bind her lover to her, even if the lover had shown some reluctance. Though as her father employed him and moreover was handy with his fists, William Thomas George soon came round.

Besides, you could tell he was fond of Sarah-Ann in spite of not wanting to tie himself down so young; and he had gone to the altar and even left Manchester with really very little protest. Some bewilderment perhaps there was and regret at having to leave his whole family behind. There would be opportunities in Birmingham, said her father, proffering the carrot along with the stick. He boasted of knowing the place well, having lived there for over ten years, her own first ten years.

Still wandering, she wished she knew the place as well as he. It was dinnertime now, or would have been had she been at home. Suddenly and with a rush of certainty, it came to her: she *must* find home. It was truly her only hope. Perhaps he had changed his mind, once the storm of anger had passed, once he had stopped roaring about gone-to-the-bad and asylums and hell-fire and workhouses and whores and disgrace, once he began to think rationally of her fate.

If only her mother had been alive. She, small but determined, had been able to manage her husband. She would not have seen her daughter thrown out on the streets whatever she had done. A few more tears dropped.

She tried to push away the panic and think calmly. At least the rain had stopped and the sun was gradually drying her clothes. She gazed about her, at the street now thronged with folk bustling about their myriad errands. She was lost, but she at least knew the name of the street where they had rented the house. She also remembered their arrival some six weeks ago at the grand station and the route they had taken out of town. She had, she thought, gaining some command over herself, been up and down local streets several times a week. She must sooner or later spot a landmark, some shop, some street-name that she recognised.

A woman in bonnet and shawl, a respectable-looking, matronly woman holding a small boy by the hand, approached. Eliza stopped in front of her. The woman's face grew stony as if suspecting a beggar, or a trick of some kind.

'Excuse me Ma'am,' said Eliza. 'Could you tell me the way to Park Road, please?'

The woman shook her head and made as if to move on. Eliza knew she must look a wretched creature, bonnetless, hair in a tangle, bedraggled and damp.

'Or Hockley Hill?' she said, remembering that their present house was only half a mile or so from the scene of her earliest childhood. He had told her that when they had arrived in Park Road.

The woman's face cleared and she pointed. 'Canna rightly tell yo all the ways. But go on down there till yo meets the big road, turn right, go on a bit an' ask again,' she said.

'Thank you kindly Ma'am,' said Eliza. She managed a smile.

It must be early evening. She was weary, her feet half-numb from walking in the thin, indoor shoes she had been wearing when her father had thrust her out of the door into the street, and shouted that he wanted never to set eyes on her again. Did he still mean that? She would have to try, just try, to win him round. Perhaps if he saw her, hungry, tired, draggle-tailed, his heart might melt?

He had always, until lately, been a just father; a no-nonsense father certainly, but she knew she had pleased him, had known he was fond of her although she was only a daughter and not the son she knew he wanted. There had been a son once, twice even, maybe more if all house-moves could be read as disappointments in that line. There had been times too, when her mother had been inexplicably 'ill'. She could remember at least one baby brother. She had been four perhaps, could just recollect a brother with a name, John, after their father. The baby had learnt to gurgle, smile and crawl; and there'd been joy in her father's eyes as he encouraged him. Then had come grief when God, after such a short time, acquired the boy-child for Himself.

More time passed. Light was dimming. She was re-directed as to her way. Then, with a start of hope, she realised that she was on familiar ground: she had passed this way before. A shout, 'Liza! Our Liza!' made her heart spring in her chest: something familiar and caring in all this wretchedness.

She looked towards the voice; a faint lilt of Welsh with Lancashire overlay. It was William, her sister's new husband. She flew towards him.

'Liza, oh Eliza. We thought you was lost. We

thought you was drownded. We thought ... We thought, oh, terrible things.'

Hope filled her. 'Has he forgiven me? Does he want me back?'

William hesitated. 'No, Liza, 'e don't want you back. 'E's goin' on bad as before. An' we canna stand it. We've decided, all on us. We's goin' back to Manchester.'

'But the baby? Only... what? Nine days old! And Sarah-Ann, is she strong enough? To travel? She's not properly up yet.'

'We thinks so. Sarah-Ann, she's so cross, I've not seen her so cross, never. She an' your father, they're at it mornin' till night. I tell you, she's a brave woman, that sister o' yourn. I'll go anywhere, do anythin' to get a bit of peace. Now, we canna go this night, we'll go tomorrow, so thee'll 'ave to stay outside another night. But round the back, there's a nook I've come across where thee'll be safe as houses. An' I s'll bring thee food an' drink an' a blanket an' that. We s'll pack up all tha clothes an' bits an' all ours an' we'll be away tomorrow.'

'What about Diana?'

'She'll come, she wants to come. She can look after thee, she says, an' the babby, when it comes. Dunna pull that face. She knows. How could she 'elp knowing, wi' all the rows goin' on and such terrible things said an' all?'

'But she's only thirteen!'

'Thirteen's as good an age to know as any. An' she's goin' to know soon enough, ain't she?'

'What'll we do, though? How are we goin' to live?'

'We s'll talk about that tomorrow. I've money enough for the train, thank the good Lord. For we canna stay here an' that's a fact. An' thank the good Lord I've found thee! At first we thought as you'd be back. Then Sarah-Ann sent me to look for 'ee. She couldna come 'erself, like, 'cause of the babby. An' I've 'ad to tell the old man as I were goin' out for a pint or two, or some such. An' today I'd lost hope, just about, an' I'd turned for home, just come down that street there, an' then, there you was.' He held her arm to give support. He was a good-hearted lad, thought Eliza, gratefully.

Home was reached, such as it was and such a short time had they been there that there was still a strangeness to it.

The houses on Park Road would, a decade ago, have been each the home of a single family, the wage-earners artisans: brushmakers, shoemakers, pearl button turners, watchcase springers, makers of gold chains, brass founders and electro platers. Many of them still were.

But other houses, including their own, had become dwellings of multiple occupation. Instead of enjoying the space in families of twos and fives, numbers in each house had risen to eight and nine and more, many of them lodgers. And, to cram in more, some plots of land had been taken over, to be filled with two, three, six houses behind.

Her father had found the house, a portion of a house, where they had squashed themselves in as best they could. 'Rent's cheap while I find work,' he said. 'Beggars canna be choosers.'

Sarah-Ann had had the baby in that house, with the help of a neighbour- woman called Mrs Ward.

Mrs Ward was a monthly nurse but could add

midwifery when called upon. She lived down the road, at
No.459.

No.459 was divided into two, one section
containing an electro plate worker, his wife, four children
and a couple of lodgers. The other part contained Mrs
Ward's mother who, they were told, Mrs Ward being a
woman inclined to impart information whether asked for
it or not, had been a milk dealer before turning to school-
teaching. As well as the mother, the house was nicely
filled by Mrs Ward, her six children and a further couple
of lodgers. Behind No.459 were five other houses, filling
what had once been a garden.

They had found Mrs Ward through an
advertisement in the *Birmingham Mail*. 'Monthly Nurse,
long experience; good references; can take engagements
up to the end of June.' She had been a great help and very
comforting to Sarah-Ann; and Sarah-Ann was duly
grateful.

Their father was grateful too. Rather too grateful,
his daughters had thought resentfully.

'Still, our mam's been dead a year an' a half now,'
Sarah-Ann had said, ever the down-to-earth one. 'An' he's
a man after all, ain't 'e? An' don't you look at me like that,
Eliza Kirby,' she went on, sharply. 'All buttoned up.''

'She's a motherly soul, I'll grant,' Eliza had
answered, flushing. 'Don't come up to our mam though.'

No one would come up to their mother, the girls
all believed. She it was who had held the family together
with her good sense and her humour, chivvying their
father out of moroseness, bringing cheerfulness to
whatever job was at hand, from blacking a range to
turning a collar.

'He's always doing this an' that for that Mrs Ward,' Eliza had said, resentfully, 'Sorting out that coalman when he delivered short weight. Or she said he did, anyhow. Who's to know? Should have thought one of those hulking great lads of hers could a done that.'

'An' that's half the trouble,' Sarah-Ann had answered. 'Our father's right taken wi' all them lads. Our mam didna come up to scratch there. An' that Mrs Ward, she's got a whole building firm in the making.'

'Come on, be fair now,' had put in William, 'There's only Frank that's workin'. The other three lads, they're still at school.'

'An' where's Mr Ward?' had said Eliza, re-iterating an oft-posed question. 'Why isn't he there helping his Missis?'

'Ain't nobody seen a Mr Ward,' said Sarah-Ann. 'An' his missis is very peculiarly quiet on that subject. But there must a been one, else where did all those children come from?' She giggled.

That conversation had taken place the week before. Now they were here, approaching the site of their own house.

'Keep back now, our Liza,' said William. 'I dunna want 'im to catch sight o' thee. I s'll go an' let Sarah-Ann know I've found thee an' in a bit I'll come out wi' the blanket an' that food an' drink. Now look you, I'll show thee the nook I've found.'

He set off down the alley which led past the doors of back-houses, crossed a street and on until he came to where there must once have existed a garden, for the builder had neglected to remove the lower trunk of a tree which now formed part of a boundary: perhaps lack of time or fear of expense had stopped him from uprooting this massive bastion of vegetation. William indicated a narrow gap between tree and adjoining wall. Squeezing through, Eliza found a fissure in the hollow trunk, giving onto a small nest floored by beaten earth. A candle stub was stuck in the ground. A rusty tin cup lay on its side.

'Expect the childer come here,' William said. 'But tha should be safe enough over the night. Now, make thyself at 'ome bach an' I s'll come back soon as I can wi' the food an' that.'

He started off back up the alley while Eliza settled herself down on the earth. She felt the burn of her swollen feet and took off her shoes. She ruffled the floor with her fingers. It was dry and dusty. Good. Any rain would probably not reach her.

There was just enough room to lean her back against the inside of the trunk and stretch her legs in front of her. There would be enough room to curl into a ball, too. And just possibly, by utilising the widest stretch, she might lie down. That would be wonderful: she would await the blanket. She prayed that no other destitute looked on this cranny as home, at least for tonight.

She listened, in hope of hearing William's footsteps coming back. She could hear something animal – a cat? A rat? - rustling a little, distant voices of children, heavy wheels passing on the road.

She must have fallen asleep, was awoken by William's low voice.

"Ere's a basket. Thee'll find things in it. An' 'ere's a blanket.' He pushed a roll through the gap. 'Sorry I've been that long. I 'ad to keep 'im busy, talkin' over the job as we've got on whiles Sarah-Ann put the things together. We 'aven't told 'im yet - as we're goin', like. Tell 'im tomorrow last thing we do, an' we'll be gone.'

He disappeared. Left to herself Eliza investigated the basket. There was a tall bottle of tea which she savoured, first in gulps, then sips, reluctantly stopping herself after two-thirds of it and firming back the cork. There was an onion rough-cut into slices, a hunk of cheese, two doorsteps of bread bound with pickle and two more doorsteps plastered together with jam. She thought of the story of the Israelites in the desert and the manna given by God.

She wanted to thrust the whole meal into her mouth, but made herself nibble off small pieces, chewing many times to prolong the taste. It was bliss. She made herself leave half the jam sandwich for the morning. Then she curled into the blanket. But she would have to find a dunny, or just a hidden spot. Best, she thought, in dusk-light when she would not be seen fully, to be wondered about. She waited as long as she could while the light faded; and wriggled out.

Back again she rolled herself up, stretched full length and sank into blessed sleep.

2
1880
FLEEING NORTH

Eliza opened her eyes to a dimness, a breath of cool air on her face, unaccustomed dips and knobbles beneath her body. Her limbs ached with stiffness and there was the pain of bruises, but less than before. Memory returned. She must get up, be ready when they came. First she should visit a dunny – not their own, for fear of discovery - and use a pump to sluice her hands and face, before other folk began to stir. When she returned, all in a hurry, her hiding place lay undisturbed and no-one waited impatiently for her.

Someone, probably Sarah-Ann, had put a hairbrush into the last night's basket. She unpinned the coils of hair, their chestnut colour inherited from her mother, making a little pile on her lap of the metal pins. She set to work with the brush, made her fingers into a comb and pulled them through over and over, brushing the while until she could feel no tangles. Boys had easy lives, she thought, when it came to hair. A boy could arrange his hair in a twinkling. Hers took time.

She fretted about what possessions the others would be able, or be thoughtful enough, to bring with them. There were her clothes, and her trinket-box back in the house. Sturdy shoes were important, her other, warmer shawl.

What was the time, she wondered, alerting herself for the sound of striking clocks. She might well hear All Saints from here.

Tuesday morning: her father would be up early as always for work. What would the others do? Sarah-Ann might be able to keep herself out of the way, on the excuse of attending to the baby. Someone, Diana probably, would make sure he had his breakfast and a bit of bait to take with him. Then he would be off, expecting his son-in-law to go too. But his son-in-law would not be going. How could that be managed without a mighty row?

She would have to leave it to them. She drank the last cold third of the bottle of tea from the night before; and ate the rest of the jam sandwich, curling now with dryness.

At last she heard steps approaching.

'Eliza?' It was Sarah-Ann, urgent, anxious.

'How did you manage? What did he say? Was he very angry?'

'Just come, cariad, for now.' That was William, behind his wife, urgent too, pleading.

She crawled out of her hiding-place, bringing the basket with her.

'E' don't know as yet. I told 'im as I 'ad to register the babby an' I'd catch up wi' him in an hour. 'E wasna pleased, growled a bit, but said well, it 'ad to be done, an' 'e left. Let's be on our way afore 'e changes 'is mind or summat.'

So his courage had failed. Eliza was unsurprised. Maybe it was for the best: by the subterfuge they would have avoided an explosion of invective or worse.

William and Diana were laden with bundles, amorphous lumps tied up in blankets, their ends slung over a shoulder. Sarah Ann had the baby in a sling and bags over her arm.

'Did you remember my trinket box?' Eliza queried.

Sarah-Ann nodded and William put Eliza's bundle in front of her. 'In there, somewheres.'

'Did you bring my good shoes?'

Sarah-Ann pointed. 'Hurry.' Eliza scrabbled through the bundle, found them, put them on.

They set off walking, Eliza tentatively at first, but then with confidence, finding her feet relieved by a night's rest and sturdy footwear. They made their way towards the nearest point where a horse tram ran towards the centre of town and New Street Station. The distance was over three miles, William said, and added gallantly, too far for his wife, early risen from child-bed, to walk with the baby. But he hummed nervously as he spoke and clinked the coins in his pocket.

'We'll walk,' Eliza said. 'Me an' Diana, we can walk. We'll meet at the station entrance. Just tell us the way.'

'We'll take the most o' the bundles wi' us then,' said William, looking relieved.

They waited together until the tram arrived, when the two laden travellers climbed inside and Eliza and Diana set off on foot for town. There was a broad road to follow. Besides, there were the tramlines to guide them. Eliza felt none of the panic and confusion of the previous day. She linked arms, gratefully, affectionately, with her sister.

By the time they reached the grand entrance, they were, as their mother might have said, with a wry smile, 'gently glowing'. The sun had become quite hot and they were glad to enter the shadow of the echoing space. It was not long before they spotted their companions against a wall, William standing and gazing around him, Sarah-Ann sitting on one of the bundles, her shawl hiding most of herself and the child. Eliza realised she must be trying to surreptitiously nurse the babby. She shuddered. She was glad the sight was hidden.

All was bustle and noise. William said he was leaving them while he went to buy tickets. The babby was put over a shoulder, where it drooped, eyes closed, a milky trail dribbling from its mouth. Sarah-Ann swayed to and fro, murmuring to it and patting its back gently. It hiccupped. Eliza, in distaste, looked away at the crowds surging in and out and around.

Diana was staring at the baby with fascination. Eliza wondered if she remembered their sister, the one who had lived long enough to be christened, but not much after that.

'Do you remember Mary, our sister?' she asked. 'She arrived soon after we first went to Manchester, from Wolverhampton where you were born.'

Diana shook her head.

A Victorian Miss

She'd have been about two, thought Eliza. Too young for memories probably. *She* could remember though. And remember the sadness in the house, even though they all told each other that Mary had gone to Heaven where she would be very happy. Her mother had lost her spirits for some time after that. And had become very worried that neither Sarah-Ann nor Diana had as yet been christened and had 'had them done' together at St. John's that December; for they had moved again in the months after Mary died, as they always did after a misery.

They had not left Manchester, nor even the district, Hulme, but had changed from 10 Thomas Street in the parish of Holy Trinity where Mary had been christened and buried, to 24 Caroline Street in the parish of St. John.

Eliza had clear memories of Caroline Street where they had stayed for several years: at fourteen she had finished her schooling there, a full-time student, not working part-time once she had reached the age of ten, as many children had to, or wanted to. It had been her wish to stay at school and that had had the blessing of both parents. Both, thought Eliza with a pang, had wanted their daughters to be educated, to climb a little higher on the ladder than themselves.

It was interesting, Eliza's thoughts rambled on, how when you were in Birmingham you said you had come from Manchester because that name had been heard of by most people there. But when you were *in* Manchester or with people who knew the place, you were much more precise; and could talk of Hulme or Ardwick with folk who knew what you were on about.

A thought came, returning her to the present. 'But you

19

haven't registered the baby,' she said.

'We can do that when we're settled back in Manchester,' said her sister. 'An' we've thought of a name,' she went on. 'Eliza-Ann. What dost think? Eliza for our mam an' you; an' Ann because it sounds good an' it's a bit of my name an' it's for our Shrewsbury Gran as well.'

Eliza nodded. 'I like it,' she said, to please her sister mostly, while at the same time knowing that she didn't care what the creature's name might be; and hoping that she wouldn't have to do anything for it, the babby. Or any babby, for that matter. Ever.

Her father's reception of the news of that recent birth returned to her mind. 'Another ------ girl,' he'd said. And taken himself off to drown his sorrows. Maybe the disappointment had still been rankling when her own news had come out; and had helped to fuel some of his outrage.

She thought back: he hadn't always been so bad-tempered, reacting with such force to anything which displeased him. One of her earliest memories was of riding on his shoulders, both fearful and safe at the same time, laughing. And another time when they'd all gone on a train journey and walked through tall, prickly grass and taken off boots and socks to paddle together in water which ran cold and clear over pebbles. She remembered once reaching up to hold his big, rough hand while they watched showers of colour snapping and twinkling against a dark sky. He had not always been so black-browed and fearsome.

She closed her eyes.

When she came up out of sleep, the train was still

beating its rhythmic tattoo.

'Are we getting near?' she asked. Sarah-Ann was asleep. Diana was cradling the baby, who was also asleep.

William answered. 'Be about half an hour.'

'Where shall we go then?' She had been dreading this, trying not to think of the answer.

William looked at her as if she were daft. 'Home, o' course. Where else could us go?'

'Ardwick, you mean?' She watched the telegraph wires swooping and rising.

'Course I mean Ardwick. They'll be a bit surprised, but our mam'll be so pleased to see the babby, it'll be huggin' an' kissin' for all of us, hugs a bundle. An' tomorrow I s'll find a job an' we'll look for our own place.'

Manchester's Central Station came at last and they set out for Ardwick. For there was to be found Swindell's Buildings, which was where William had lived till his wedding only five months ago; lived with his parents, a brother or two and a couple of sisters.

Swindell's Buildings was a group of five houses, built and owned by the Midland Railway. The railway was so close that it could not be ignored and the area had spawned a coalyard and a whole herd of sheds of mysterious usage. The house was meagre.

The only person at home was Mrs George. She stared blankly for a moment as they came in, dropped the potato knife she was holding, erupted into a stream of Welsh and hugged them all.

'Sit you, sit you,' she said and more Welsh erupted. The babby was exclaimed over, first in Welsh and then in

English, the kettle lifted from the tiny fire and poured onto leaves of tea.

'One thing we do have, diolch i Dduw, is the coal,' she said, gesturing towards the fire. 'Pick it up from the coalyard, see. An' they turns a blind eye 'cause of Mr George working for the railway. Now, you tell me all about yourselves, fy annwyl.'

William began an explanation, in part and halting Welsh, during which Mrs George's eyes flicked from one to another. When they rested on Eliza a frown came to her forehead and she shook her head slowly and tightened her mouth a little. But there came compassion in her eyes and she got up from her chair, came over and put an arm round the girl's shoulders.

'You are not the first and you will not be the last, cariad.' And she murmured a phrase in which Eliza caught 'Dduw' again.

They would stay at least one night, it was confirmed. They would have to sleep wherever they could lay themselves down and eat what was to offer. But they were welcome.

The workers began to come in at a quarter after seven, depending how far they had to walk from their place of work. Mr George was first, being a drayman employed by the Railway and his stabling being on the premises. Ann and Fanny did factory work. The last to arrive was a larger version of William, who took one startled look at the new arrivals, muttered something and turned towards the door.

A sharpness of Welsh brought him back, to shake hands with his brother, nod to Sarah-Ann and Eliza, and peek reluctantly at the babby. Then he was gone.

A Victorian Miss

His mother looked to the ceiling, spread her two hands in the air, palms upwards.

The next morning, they set off northwards; or rather William, Eliza and Diana set off, leaving Sarah-Ann and the babby at home with Mrs George.

'Thee'll have to work,' had been agreed the night before, when all but the still-absent brother had been apprised of Eliza's situation. Heads had been dourly shaken, mouths pursed, but no appalled and righteous indignation had been openly expressed.

'Nothing shows, Eliza bach, an' wi' the right clothes an' it being tha first ...' the mother said.

'An' tha can be a widow-woman,' said Anne, the older of the two sisters.

'An' Diana, she'll have to work an' all,' put in Fanny, who was rather younger than Diana and already working as a machinist.

'Ancoats'll likely be the best place,' said Mr George, tapping a thoughtful finger on the table. 'Plenty of places to work in Ancoats, plenty of places to live, an' cheap too.'

Which is why William, Eliza and Diana were walking across the city very early on a hot July morning. Ancoats would suit her well, thought Eliza: there was someone she knew in Ancoats. She twisted her mother's wedding ring, abstracted from her trinket box, round and round the third finger of her left hand. She was dressed in the most sombre clothes she had, remnants of the mourning she had donned for that mother.

'I'm for the dyeworks,' said William, when they'd neared their destination. 'You go on to Murray's Mills in

Union Street. Cotton mills. Always lookin' for workers. An' they're not above using women. Mostly do, anyhow; 'cause they be cheaper, o' course.'

A surly man wearing a waistcoat and with his dirty shirt-sleeves rolled above his elbows, interviewed the girls briefly, told them the hours, 'Six to six. Six to half twelve Saturdays. Two hour for meals. Latecomers locked out. Lose wages. Keep doin' it, lose't job. No call for 'ands right now. Come back next week.'

They walked away. The streets were set in a grid pattern and they made mental notes as they went along, trying to keep track of the names. Each street was the grim twin of the next, a line of identical houses on each side, opening directly onto the cobbles, a window to the side of the door, a window above. All were fashioned of soot-blackened brick, all had chimneys from which coal-smoke curled, or which promised to curl later when the inhabitants came home from work.

Mills of three, seven or even eight storeys sat heavily here and there, dwarfing the houses, casting them into shadow; and above each mill complex towered its own giant chimney, billowing its vastly superior oily blackness into the air.

Another cotton mill hove into sight, proclaiming its owner and his business in tall, white lettering high on the facade. They asked again about work and wages. The answer was much the same but, 'Start six Thursday,' they were told.

'Best us find somewhere to live,' said Eliza.

A Victorian Miss

They crossed the River Medlock: more blackness, this time the rich, thick blackness of stinking water, iridescent here and there, humps of nameless things floating.

They walked down the nearest street. This terrace of houses, each opening its single door onto a narrow pavement, would be backed by a windowless wall the length of the street. And that blank wall, topped with a single row of close-packed chimneys, would serve as the back wall of a line of mirror-dwellings, each with its only door opening onto an enclosed courtyard. A notice in a window said 'LOGINS TO LET.'

Eliza knocked. They were admitted directly from the street into the one dim and airless room that constituted the downstairs, with the most meagre of windowless scullery arrangements at its back. Nameless clutter surged around their feet. They could hear muffled voices. They both looked round, seeing no-one, before realising that the voices came from behind the party-wall.

Out of the room rose the stairs, leading to the one bedroom above. It was the attic, a storey higher, that was to let, explained a sharp-faced six-year-old hefting a baby who chewed at a rag, grizzling the while. The privies were round the back, she said. 'Down't street, through't passage. Wash-'ouse there an all.' Her parents and brother and sisters were all out at the Mill.

They exchanged glances, thanked her and moved on. Waugh Street beckoned. No.26 had 'ROOM TO LET'. Eliza's assessing glance lit on the doorstep: it had been freshly scrubbed.

They could have a furnished front bedroom for 3s.6d a week. The house had its own outdoor privy, an earth closet, emptied regularly from the alley behind by the night-soil man. They could share the range in the back room for cooking, though their landlady would provide an evening meal. There was water piped into the house.

Eliza looked at Diana. Their wages would be low at first: they would be slow and were unskilled, but that was a rent they might just afford between them. She dared not think of what would happen later.

The woman, Mrs Booth, seemed a pleasant person and the house was clean. Inside, the stench, which hung always in the air of a town, sometimes lesser, sometimes overpowering, was almost undetectable.

'We'll take it,' said Eliza firmly, and passed over a shilling. 'We'll be back tomorrow, with the baggage.'

Back in Swindell's Buildings, weary from the walking and the anxiety, Eliza longed to lie down and sleep. But people came in from their work, had to be fed, needed to talk a little, to tell the stories of their day, needed to be self-directed, individual beings for a short while at least, before oblivion, followed by mindless labour, would swallow them again.

William had found a job at the dyeworks. He had fancied trying something else, he said, something other than the bricklaying that he'd done before when he'd worked with their father. He and Sarah-Ann would be staying in Swindell's Buildings, for the short term at least.

On Thursday morning, Eliza and Diana arrived at the Mill slightly before six, in their anxiety not to fall foul of the rules. A crowd, preponderantly women, of all ages, waited outside. The gates opened: they flooded in. The sisters presented themselves at the glass window of an office, as they had been instructed; and waited, watching the while, to learn how things were done.

A man came from the door of the office, looked them over. Both women had scarves bound round their heads, but Diana was told to put her long plait down the back of her dress and Eliza to tuck her put-up hair even more tightly behind the scarf.

Women's hair, they would be told later, caught in machinery, could lead to terrible accidents.

Then he preceded them, across yards, up stairs and down long corridors, to a vast room where the noise of machinery was overwhelming and where Diana was left to the care of a weasel-faced man of middle-age and some sharpness.

Eliza was moved on, by a web of ways, to another vast room, day-lit like the first by great oblong windows divided into smaller oblong panes. All was rattle and pound, undershot by rhythm. Fibres of cotton floated as a mist. It was very warm; and not only warm but there was a dampness to it. Eliza felt herself sweating, drops oozing from her skin. The moisture anchored the fluff, which began to irritate.

She was taken, by someone whom she assumed was an overlooker, to a machine in the far reaches of the mist, sections of it rotating at high speed. A woman somewhat older than Eliza, her whole outline fuzzed palely with fluff, was in charge. By leaning towards Eliza and gesticulating and shouting, at intervals, into her ear, Eliza reached some understanding of what was happening here, though she could see the mechanism clearly only when the break came at last.

The woman had been feeding a soft, never-ending sheet of fibres into a whirling something. Now it had come to rest, Eliza could see a drum-like object. The outer surface of the drum was spiked with wires. It whirled round within a case, from the inside of which stuck out more wires.

It was between those two sets of wires, that the woman was feeding the wadding, that soft, never-ending sheet of raw cotton. It came out of the initial drum only to be whirled off through other, smaller drums, the strands becoming thinner and neater the while, in a longitudinal way.

'What's it all for?' Eliza asked, bemused.

'Meks fibres straight. Teks out bits, an' all, if as there's any left: dirt, seeds an' stalks an' stuff,' said the skinny girl on her left. 'Carding, it's called. You's a carder. Did they none tell yer?'

Eliza's instructor was using a rag to wipe away the sweat-soaked fluff from her face. 'Lines up fibres as well, so as to get strong threads. Dunna want no breakin' see, when they comes to spinnin'. Masters'd not be pleased, tha knows,' she said.

Eliza learned for the rest of that day, trying her hand here and there, and more as time went on, watched and instructed by her mentor. When the overlooker had decided she was fully competent she would be let loose on her own machine, she was told.

A list of rules was pinned to the wall, drawn to her attention by the woman under whose care she temporarily was. Many things, it seemed, were forbidden: lateness, waste, oil spilled, oiling neglected, talking, bad language when talking, being absent from the machine, walking off the job without giving four weeks' notice, damaging anything belonging to the factory, being unwashed, smoking and hanging anything on the gas jets.

Eliza looked at the gas jets. It was light enough now, due to the big windows and its being July, but in the short, dark days, the gas lights would be essential. She had a moment's unease about proximity of cotton fluff and gas jets, but it surely could be of no importance.

Six o' clock came at last. Eliza clocked off, waiting for her sister. She was weary to the bone. Diana managed a wan smile, but seemed almost too tired to walk or even talk. Neither girl had before put in such a long, intensive day. The air, when they came into the open to wipe the irritating fibres from their moist faces and forearms and spit it from their mouths, was blessedly free from cotton. But after the heat of the mill, they were glad to wrap their shawls closely about them.

The silence, too, was blessed, save that their ears still rang. And of course, it was not really silent but held a lower level of noise: rumbling of carts, the whinny of a horse; and over all, as the crowd of workers spilled forth from the mill gates, a twittering as of a thousand starlings; and a clattering, the sound of hundreds of wooden clogs striking the cobbles.

It was not far to Waugh Street and they tumbled in, to sluice themselves as best they could before they sat down to the first of Mrs Booth's meals, a meal which they silently and gratefully assessed as being just about adequate in quantity and not unflavoursome.

Too tired afterward to exchange more than a few

words, they retreated to their bed. 'Sleep the deep sleep of the just. Dost remember, Eliza?' murmured Diana; and the two sisters took comfort from the echo of their mother's voice.

That was Thursday. On the Friday morning, as they walked to work, the girls exchanged details of the previous day.

'They gave me a brush,' Diana said. 'An' I didn't know what they wanted me to do. They said, but I couldn't hear because of the noise – such a huge clatter, all the time. It makes my ears ring. Anyhow, they showed me as I had to sweep the floor. That floor was all over bits of cotton and it was in the air and it kept floating down. An' you keep brushing it up an' there it is, back again. An' the floor's big flagstones, all oily an' the fluff sticks. Oh, and Eliza, it gets stuck to your face, the cotton fluff, 'cos you're all sweaty like, 'cos it's so warm an' damp. And your eyes itch.'

Eliza soothed. What else to do? She had suffered much the same experience. 'You'll get used to it,' she said.

There was a silence. Then Diana began again. 'And then they showed me I had to reach under the machines, to reach as far under as I could with the brush an' get all the fluff out. It's so *noisy,* Eliza. I can't hardly hear myself think. And there's iron bits and they shoot back'ards and forrards so very fast. They're fierce, horrid somehow, those machines. And I don't like him, that man.

'Which man? Why?'

'That sharp-faced man, the overlooker. He shouts at me so. An' he looks at me nasty like.'

'How, nasty?' asked her sister.

'Don't know. Nasty.'

The end of Friday found each girl as tired as the day before, though perhaps a little more confident at her work.

Diana woke Eliza with her cries that night. Eliza held her and made soothing noises. 'What frightened you so?' she asked at last, but gently, stroking her sister's hair back from her face.

'I was under the mule,' Diana said, after a while, remembering,'

'Mule?'

'That's what the machines are called. And they're so big! There's a thousand spindles on them, winding the yarn.'

'So what were you doing under a mule, you silly?' Eliza asked, smiling.

'I have to, cos I'm a scavenger! The minder stops the mule and me and Ada, she's the piecer, we run under, very fast and we wipe bits as we go, a rail, a beam. You have to run bending down low or the machine might get you.'

'But you said it was stopped, the mule-thing?' asked Eliza anxiously.

'Yes, but … you keep thinking as it'll start up again. An' they say I'm big, for a scavenger, so look out. And they told me all sorts of horrid stories about times when the machine'd been started too soon and girls'd lost their hands or arms and all their hair pulled off and all the skin with it.' Diana began to cry.

'Oh, mean, nasty girls! They were only trying to frighten you! Don't you take any notice. Anyway, you got out safe, didn't you? Well, then.' There was not much else she could say. Her heart sank at the dread of it; but they had to live, had to work.

They walked on. 'We do have to wave at the minder when we're both out,' said Diana bravely after a while. 'And he waves back. Then he starts the machine again.'

'There you are then. Safe as houses,' said her sister. 'Now go back to sleep. We've to be up at five.'

It was Saturday, and Saturday was a half-day, a blessed thing. How wonderful to arrive at six, knowing that at half an hour after noon you would be free; and that last half-hour devoted only to cleaning the workplace and the machinery. And then to look forward to a glorious further whole day, Sunday, when no work awaited.

'What shall us do, Eliza?' asked Diana, when they left the mill that first Saturday afternoon.

Eliza thought. They had borrowed a little money from Mr George, on the promise of its repayment as soon as they themselves were paid. Mr Booth, through the kindly Mrs Booth, had agreed to defer half their rent until the following Saturday when they should get their first wages. They would have to find something to do which would cost nothing; but what would that be, in such a barrenness of a place?

'We could walk the canal, watch the barges maybe?' said Diana. 'Or we could go over to Ardwick, see Sarah-Ann and the baby.'

'Canals everywhere, in Ancoats,' said Eliza, who had no enthusiasm to watch boats passing; and even less to see a baby. 'The Rochdale, the Ashton, little offshoots all over. Where there's a mill, there's a bit of canal. An' there's mills enough to clothe the world in cotton, keep us in glass an' silk an' iron an' brass besides. No, I think we should go back to our lodgings, tidy up: I've a pair of stockings want washing, and a shift. Have a bit of a nap, maybe. We'll find the market later. See what we can get for bait an' such for next week, summat as we can take to the mill. We need tea; an' a loaf an' some dripping an' onions. Tomorrow'll be the day for seeing Sarah-Ann. More time then.' She supposed they would have to go, though it would be an effort she would make with reluctance.

They'd heard of, and even visited, Smithfield Market, of course, during their previous years in the town. It was large and had been there in some form or another for a very long time. Mrs Booth provided directions, so that at seven-thirty they were threading their way through the streets in the general direction of the city centre.

The building, or rather complex of buildings, was vast. Brick it was, like the rest of the town, largely enclosed, its internal roofs great arches of cast iron and glass. Below were stalls, each in its section, selling meat and fish, fruit and vegetables in profusion.

'We'll have a look about us, for now,' said Eliza. 'Take the lie o' the land. Find what there is and compare prices. Mrs Booth said wait till things get cheaper the closer it gets to ten o' clock. But then o' course, the best might have already gone.'

'Oh, look over there!' cried Diana. A monkey with soulful eyes perched on the shoulder of a hurdy-gurdy man. As they watched, it leapt away, disappeared under a stall and reappeared with a few cherries which it proceeded to eat delicately one by one.

They drifted down the aisles, trying to imprint a map into their heads. There were conjurors, fiddle-players, pavement artists who would draw your likeness on the stones for a penny or two. There were men in aprons and flat cloth caps who shouted their wares and were a joy to listen to as they persuaded you they were selling the best there was, now, ever had been and ever would be, and for the lowest of all possible prices; beggaring themselves for your especial, esteemed benefit out of the high regard they had for you.

Whole families strolled among the aisles, pointing and laughing, enjoying themselves together, the mother alert for the chance of picking up something that would make a good Sunday dinner tomorrow.

Nine o' clock came and the girls began to buy, worried in case they should lose all. Eliza was cautious about the produce. Meat that seemed altogether too much of a bargain she avoided, having learnt from her mother that it could be from an animal dead before it ever reached a slaughter-house: diseased meat. Flour of a blinding whiteness was probably more alum than flour itself. Milk of low price might well contain more chalk than anything that came out of a cow.

Most of the food was for Mrs Booth: it would be a help for them to buy it for her, save her a journey, she said. And they could have a few pennies knocked off the rent for their trouble. A brace or two of kippers they would take with them on the Sunday to Swindell's Buildings. Kippers were cheap, kept well, could be quickly cooked and they knew that the Georges had a fondness for them. For themselves and their midday meal at the mill next week, they provided themselves with those staples: bread, cheese and onions.

A Victorian Miss

It was a glittering, entertaining evening; and best of all, apart from those few, necessary purchases, it was free.

3
1880
BUCKLING TO

The cotton came into the mill tied in bales, like hay. The bales came in by waterway. From the great port of Liverpool, the bales were transported down the windings of the River Mersey, then by narrow canal, then the River Irwell, and another, shorter distance by canal again. It was a route gradually becoming impassable, silting up more each year.

Something would have to be done, they said, the mill owners and the powers-that-be. A much more efficient canal would have to be built; adding that yes, the railway was there as an alternative but ruinously expensive.

The cotton had reached Liverpool by travelling thousands of miles across the sea from America, where it had been grown largely by people of darker hue who had until recently been slaves, though were no longer.

Sometimes, in Church, where Eliza had been sent on

many a Sunday, there had been missionaries who had told them about the hard lives of people with dusky skins who were now learning of kindly, Christian ways; and Eliza had been glad to think of her penny going across the seas to help them.

She thought of this as she fed her thin wadding of raw cotton into the carding machine in the twelfth hour of her working day. Some of those kindly Christian ways applied to the lives of mill-girls here at home might not come amiss.

It was men's work, the 'opening', hauling the huge bales from the barges into the ground floor of the mill and untying them, taking out the pods of cotton, ridding them of their coverings. It was heavy work and it was hot work and in the steamy atmosphere of the mill, good for cotton, bad for people, the men worked half-naked.

'Oh, there's no women work in there,' the mill-girls told Eliza, giggling, pretending to be outraged. 'You'd be 'avin' them ungodly thoughts if as you saw 'em all wi' nowt on. Tempted, you'd be. Can't be 'avin' none o' that.'

Unwanted things came mixed up with the cotton - dried leaves, small stones, feathers, stalks, seeds and dust. After much of it had been picked out, different bales were blended together. Then the cotton, full of clumps, was blown, puffed out, into a uniform fluff.

It then went to the scutching room where wooden rollers pounded it into a sheet of thin wadding, which they called the 'lap'. It was now a roll, three feet long, nine inches across.

The lap came in skips to the carding room, which was where Eliza first set her eyes upon it. The lap was what she fed into the drum of her machine. From there she could see it being drawn through the wires, which acted rather like brushes in disentangling the fibres of the cotton and drawing it out in threads. At the end, it came out as a long and continuous band of fleece an inch wide and a quarter inch thick. The band coiled itself into a metal drum and, now many times its original length, was given a new name, a 'roving'.

The work took a toll on her body: at night she wanted little more than a meal and bed. She had to keep her wits about her while she worked, not dream too much. The machines intimidated her with their size and their enormous, heartless strength: though at least now, by law and after too many manglings, guards had been placed between inexorable iron and fragile flesh and bone.

The brutes had to be oiled regularly so that they performed at their best. And she soon found that it was the health of the machines that took priority over the comfort of the operative. Machines were far more costly than their minders.

For the minders there was a closet in each room; and a bucket or two of water for washing. Breakfast was allowed half an hour. Dinner-time was given a whole hour, which could be spent in the mill or elsewhere. Mothers with young babies often took advantage of this to go home, usually only a few streets distant, and suckle them. A further half-hour came later.

Eliza overheard a group of women making coarse comments about unwanted babies who were not mother-fed. 'Godfrey's keeps 'em quiet. Then they just fades away. Don't suffer. Too young to know.' Could this be a solution to her own problem when the time came? She did not want this thing, this creature that was growing inside her. She knew that mother's milk was essential to nurture an infant. The substitutes that people tried, of cow's, of donkey's, of goat's milk, of bread or flour soaked in water, none of them met with great success. Perhaps she could feed it those, or Godfrey's, supposing it survived its birth? Which babies often did not, she reminded herself.

She had had those shameful, immoral thoughts, thoughts such as the naked torsos of the men in the warehouse might inspire. Except that, at the time, the thoughts, actions rather, seemed wondrous, beautiful. She knew exactly when the thing within her had been conceived, for there had been no other time.

It had been a month after her sister's wedding, almost to the day. She had first met him there, at the wedding, a man of a good height without being a bean-pole and well-built, pleasant-faced if not exactly handsome. But what had attracted her most was his humour. He had made her laugh. And his way of speaking was not smutty, nor poking fun at others' misfortunes, but generous, as if he liked people. He seemed to have a wide tolerance of character. And then, she had never been taken notice of by a young man before. She had been smitten. And life for a little while, inventing excuses for being out of the house while secretly meeting him, had taken on an intensity where colours seemed brighter, happenings more significant, happiness welling up from below and radiating through her dull life.

For dull it was. After she had left school, her father had not wanted her to find paid work as many girls did, as

Sarah-Ann had done for a while before she became a married woman. But Sarah-Ann, the younger sister and the less obedient, had insisted and sulked and thrown tantrums until her father gave in. All she had been was a parlourmaid in a pretty apron, but she had at least seen the comfortable, alien world of the gentry and earned a little money that was her own, she said.

Eliza had given in to parental wishes. Her father was proud of being able to support wife and daughters without their having to go out to work. So Eliza stayed at home and learnt household skills; which would stand her in good stead, said her father, when she came to get a husband. The downside, thought Eliza, was that potential husbands did not knock the door of wherever they happened to be living at the time, and ask to come a-courting the bricklayer's daughter. True, William George had found Sarah-Ann the bricklayer's daughter, but more because he was a bricklayer himself and had reasons to call. And she, Eliza, was beginning to dread the prospect of yet another birthday - it would be her twenty-fourth - and no young man a-calling, not even a bricklayer.

The housekeeping education had been useful when her mother sickened and died. But then, she suspected, her father had seen her as a replacement for her mother, someone who would carry on the excellent care her mother had provided, would look after him as he grew old. He would never want for household comforts, would simply pursue his life as he liked to lead it, tended by the most dutiful of daughters. It must have come as a most dreadful shock to him, the realization that this easy life was to be disintegrated, and most shamefully; first by Sarah-Ann's shattering the aura of family respectability, followed by herself compounding the explosion.

Her stomach was expanding. She knew this from feeling it when she was in bed. If she looked at herself in the glass when dressed, twisting to show the side view, she could see almost no difference. But there would be a change soon, no matter how tightly she laced. It was better, she had begun to think, to do the opposite. The conclusion had come about by accident, for the mill was so hot and humid that she had taken to loosening her dress and had found that a bump was not so noticeable. And, dress topped with the voluminous, gathered apron which she wore at work, she might deceive for a while yet.

She had, taking her niece Anne's advice, passed herself off from the first, both to the Booths and to those at the mill, as the widowed Mrs Kirby. Being unknown in Ancoats, she remained unchallenged. About her husband, if quizzed, she said as little as possible, deflecting questions, hypocritically dabbing her eyes, and changing the subject. After all, an accident at work, the death of a young husband, was not uncommon.

Time passed; a few weeks. On Saturday nights she and Diana visited the Smithfield Market, always a scene of liveliness. People enjoyed themselves, were in a good humour there: the workers had been paid that day and had a little money to rattle in their pockets, a few spare coins over which, for one evening at least, they had lordly choice of disposal.

Occasionally, of a Saturday afternoon, they walked the pavements of Deansgate, of Corporation or Exchange Streets in the city, to gaze at things beyond their reach: chairs from America, carved furniture from Delhi, chimney glasses, pianofortes, sealskin mantles at 13 guineas, cloaks of black cashmere lined with squirrel-fur at 59s.6d, spun-silk jersey dresses for evening wear, dinner services for twelve persons incorporating vast tureens, paper hangings, linoleum which was the up-to-the-minute way of flooring and so very easy to clean. Their wages were regular now and had risen a little with competence, but only in dreams would they wear a fur-lined mantle.

Eliza had early on tried jumping from chairs, running, falling - she had hurt an ankle and limped for a few days - even an excess of gin, but nothing had been of avail. The Thing continued to grow.

One night she felt an odd sensation, as of a stirring, a fluttering and she found herself suddenly weeping. The Thing had announced its presence and, even as she was bitter in resentment of this proof of material existence, she found she could not hate it as wholly as before.

She looked through newspapers, usually the cumbrously-named *Manchester Courier and Lancashire General Advertiser*, the '*Courier*' for short. In the small ads, alongside advertisements for dog-kennels, stoves and left-off clothing, she came across 'Respectable Widow, with comfortable Home, wants Baby or young Child to nurse.' There were many of these, she noted. Were they, though, quite what they seemed? She had heard the ominous term 'baby farm'. A way out, said part of her, while another part asked could she do that to a tiny creature, no matter how impossible its life was going to make hers?

There were, she noted, places for 'homeless and

destitute children', like the Boys and Girls Refuge at Strangeways.

A baby was deposited at the door of the Board of Guardians.

Another was left in a hamper outside the door of a respectable gentleman, the mother soon traced as having been his dismissed maidservant. Eliza toyed with the latter idea, of dumping it on its father. But a small and tiresome voice inside her niggled that this seemed somehow unkind to an innocent child: it might take cold, or be ravaged accidentally by a famished hound ... And if she left the child with its father, would not the truth come out, as it had in this reported case? And she recoiled from having to admit to being a mother without a husband: it was too shaming. Besides, even if the father did acknowledge the child and made her his wife, she was coming to the painful realisation that she may have been in love as much with love itself and with being admired, as with the boy. The prospect of being tied to him for life had, over time, turned from desirable to problematic to distinct disinclination.

Thus far she had resisted all pleas and threats, even those of her father, to reveal the child's paternity. She could not bring herself to do that. She wondered if he had guessed by now? Surely he must have done. But time had shown there would be no help from that quarter and she would want nothing from him. It would certainly provide a way out, but no, she did not want him. Which was just as well, because she was certain by now that he did not want her either. She felt she was in a trap and wriggle as she might, there was only one painful course to take. There was a person, though, to whom she might talk.

The following Saturday afternoon after work finished, she left Diana on her own to tend to odd jobs. She walked down Waugh Street into Russell Street, turned left down to where Palmerston Street crossed its end; and looked for No.148. Why she had not done this before she could not untangle, only knew that she had been reluctant. The friend, Sarah, must imagine her to be still in Birmingham with the rest of the family; and presumably safe and well.

Eliza knocked. Sarah opened the door, a moment of incomprehension, then recognition and surprise. She flung her arms round Eliza, full of exclamations.

'I thought thee were in Birmingham! Why's thee back 'ere? Ar't alright? Tha looks peaky. Come on in, me duck. Sit thee down. Tell us all about it.'

Eliza found tears welling and shook them away.

'Now don't 'ee fret. Joe's out on a job an' it must be finished. An' the little uns won't mind thee.' Two little boys looked at Eliza shyly and went back to playing with a lump of clay.

The tangle of emotions exploded. 'We left so quickly, such a hurry. Father took us off so soon, soon as he found out about Sarah-Ann. An' I didn't know then. If I had I'd've come an' told you. But there wasn't time. An' I couldn't write. How could I have said? An' now we're back an' I don't know what to do.'

The pent-up anguish spewed forth, while Sarah cuddled her and made soothing noises. The little boys looked up, startled, and gazed for a few moments before going back to their clay.

Little by little, Sarah questioned her way through the muddle until she knew the main strands of the story. 'But who's the father?' she asked at last, puzzled.

There was a silence. 'Alfred,' said Eliza at last. She glared at Sarah, daring her to smile.

But she said, 'Alfred, eh? I suppose you mean the brother?' And thought a while. 'And there's no chance 'e'd mek an honest woman of thee?'

'He doesn't know. Leastways, he must've guessed by now, though he's said nowt. And I'm so sorry,' Eliza went on. 'Back then I said I were with you, and all the time I was with him. Father wouldn't have let me go out if he'd known. But it wasn't fair to you an' I suppose that's why I've not come to see you, though we've been back here since just after Sarah-Ann's baby was born and that was the 25th of June.'

'And now it's September,' said Sarah. 'How far gone is thee?'

'Five months, near six.'

'Let's tek a look.'

Eliza stood up while Sarah viewed her critically. 'I can just about tell,' she said.

'I've said as I'm a widow-woman,' said Eliza.

'Well, that'll do for most folk. They'll talk, o' course, but let 'em. Now, who's going to 'elp thee? Bear the child, I mean?'

Eliza shook her head: she had no idea. 'I'm not going in the workhouse,' she said fiercely.

'No, no, o' course not,' said Sarah soothingly. 'I know of a woman near. She'll ask no questions if you pays 'er right, an' she's clean. She'll 'ave thee in 'er 'ouse for a couple of days, a week even.'

'And after that?' Eliza asked.

'After that you goes back to't mill. An' gets on best as

thee can. What about the folks thee's lodgin' with?'

'Mrs Booth? She's a kindly soul. She's three of her own, young ones. I think she might let us stay. And her husband, he's a cabinet maker, but I don't think he earns much. I think they need the money. And we're quiet, Diana and me.'

'Won't be so quiet when there's a babby,' said Sarah. And laughed.

Eliza glanced down at the little boys, all fair curls and large grey eyes. 'Well, you've got two angels,' she said.

'Don't you believe it,' said her friend, patting their heads lightly.

Sarah was older than Eliza by eight years. Her husband Joseph was a brickmaker, which was where the relationship had begun, a trade relationship with Eliza's bricklayer father. The two men had got on well as, subsequently, so had wife and daughter. Joseph was the older of the two men by more than a decade; and nearly thirty years older than his wife. Sarah was, of course, his second wife; and the two little boys were the start of his second family.

'So how'd it come about?' asked Sarah.

'Well, we were larking about an' I was feeling so happy, and it was Leap Year you know, and it had gone the 29th of February but we were full of tomfoolery and I asked him to marry me. An' he said, 'Yes cariad.' An' then, well, we were all loving and then it happened. And we weren't drunk nor nothing. And I didn't really think till afterwards. And I just hoped nothing would happen - they say it don't the first time - but it did. And then, by the time I knew like, Father was taking us all away because of

Sarah-Ann; and I never saw him again. I thought he was an older brother, see.'

'An' 'e were a younger one,' said Sarah. 'Oh, dearie, dearie me. An' you never asked 'im? 'Ow old 'e was?''

'I only found out by William talking, an' that was after. I knew William had two brothers, and this one, being so much bigger than William, I just thought he was older. William's twenty-one so I thought Alfred'd be twenty-three maybe, like me.'

'An' 'ow old is 'e, exactly?'

'Seventeen,' said Eliza, after a pause.

'Just a lad, eh?'

'And on a lad's wages. He won't want to get married at his age. And not to an old woman who's near enough on the shelf. It's ... it's disgusting. And I'd feel like that, even if we did get married ... Everyone laughing behind our backs and his mates sneering and making nasty jokes. No, I couldn't have it.'

'Joseph's a sight older than me,' said Sarah.

'But that's different somehow. People think it right, a man being older than his wife. But t'other way round and folks get laughed at. Besides, girls grow up quicker than boys do. Get more sense earlier ...Though you might say I don't fit that bill,' she added, flushing. 'Oh, what I'd give to undo things!'

'So, you'll be lyin'-in December time,' said Sarah. 'I'll go round to this woman I knows of. She looked after me neighbour, last month, so I knows you can trust 'er. Not like some. Now what about a layette?'

But Eliza had given no thought to what the Thing might wear, praying that it might never become actual reality.

'Suppose you don't know any more women, women that would ... You know, women that'd make it alright again?' she said tentatively.

'I don't know of nobody. An' if I did I wouldna tell thee. Likely die, doing that, you an' the babby, both. 'Sides, I may not be much of a churchgoing Christian, but I does know what's right. An' so do you, Eliza Kirby.'

Sarah had baby-clothes saved. For, as she said, Jesse might not be the last one. 'Waste not, want not' had always stood her in good stead; and the clothes would not suffer by having another little owner for a few months. Boys and girls wore much the same when newborn and for the first years, she pointed out. And, of course, Joe and Jesse grew all the time and their handed-down garments would last the baby-to-come some while. Joe, it was true, had now graduated to a sailor suit, but if Eliza's baby was a girl, well, God would provide. And then, who knows what might happen over time? She winked.

'Nobody'll want me,' said Eliza firmly, mouth down-turned in self-distaste. 'What man wants a girl who's spoiled; and for all to see, when she's lumbered with another man's child? Only a poor, decrepit half-man at best, as can't expect anyone better,' she answered herself. 'No. I shall be a spinster to the end o' my days.' Her eyes watered.

'Now, Eliza Kirby, pull thysen together. We'll not go looking for misfortune. The good Lord will provide, as the Bible tells us.'

Eliza, walking the short distance back to Waugh Street, her secret shared at last, more calm that she had been for some while, felt her courage revived. Somehow she would overcome the dreadful mess that she had, with one short act, made of her whole future life. There would come a time, she thought, with a new determination, a day would come when she would again be respectable. Respectable was what you strove to be, to be regarded as, by all those around you.

She noticed that No.34 Waugh Street, a step away, was 'To Let'; and made a mental note to tell Sarah-Ann and William the following day. Life was far too cramped for them in Swindell's Buildings, William wanted to be nearer the dyeworks and, having now saved and begged enough to acquire the bare essentials, they were ready to move into a home of their own with the babby. It would be good to have them living only a few doors away. It could be helpful when the Thing finally arrived. But she had rather not think of that.

Walking over to the Georges' that Sunday, they were waylaid by someone unexpected.

'You go on ahead to the house,' said Eliza to her sister. 'Here, take this.' She handed Diana the basket with dripping and bread bought the night before in the market. 'I'll not be long behind.'

Diana scurried off obediently, leaving the two alone together. They stood awkwardly apart.

'Eliza, cariad.'

Cariad. The word rent her heart. With that rose a flame of searing resentment. If people knew that Alfred had fathered a child, they'd call him a rascal, maybe. But they'd likely give him a forgiving clap on the shoulder at the same moment, or smile with a mix of reproof and admiration. Or say the poor fellow had been bewitched.

But by doing the same thing, she was nothing but an object of disgust. Why were things so different for women? But that was how it was.

'Eliza. Was it me?'

She stared at him, at this moment a lumbering lad, awkward, shuffling, hangdog; stared haughtily, without deigning to reply.

He looked at his feet. 'I never meant to. It just happened, tha knows.'

'I know. What's done is done.'

'I can give thee a little. From my wages. To tide thee over when the babby comes. An' soon as I can I s'll get a better job. I'm thinking to join the City Police.'

'And when will that be, Alfred George?'

'S'posed to be twenty-one, but I'll try earlier.'

'And have a row of shiny buttons all down your front? And a helmet with a peak and a shiny knob on top? And carry a truncheon? And change that belt-buckle you're so proud of for another?

Alfred flushed. 'Now come, Eliza, just because ... Anyways, they likes them as been sodgers, the police do. Them as can handle a gun ain't afraid to handle a truncheon when it's needed. An' they ain't scared of a scrap neither. An' they can polish a boot. Which is worth much to a policeman. 'Cause you rises up the ladder 'cording to the brightness of your boots. An' my boots'll be pretty big uns besides.' With which he drew himself up to his full height and saluted smartly.

Eliza giggled in spite of herself. If the truth be told, she had once been rather proud of her lover's participation in the Lancashire Artillery Volunteers and his talk of 24- and 32-pounders and the 40-pounder Armstrong with a rifled breech; and his uniform which set off his well-made body; and the silver buckle which he polished to a gleaming softness.

'Well, see as you gets some stripes on your sleeve,' she said severely.

'I will that,' said Alfred, grinning. Then his smile faded. 'Who's thee told?' he enquired anxiously.

'Only Sarah, Sarah Hoskinson. And she's my friend. And she won't tell no-one,' Eliza said.

'I'll give thee what I can spare,' promised the boy. 'But after I've paid me mam, there's little left.'

'I'd be glad of a bit,' said Eliza. 'Not for myself, mind, but for the … the babby when it comes. Now, let's be moving or they'll be talking. An' no, since you so kindly ask, I don't want to marry thee, not one bit I don't.'

4
1880
IT SHALL COME TO PASS

The mill-girls reacted in various ways to Eliza's expanding girth. When they were eating their hunks of bread, swigging their tea, she caught sideways looks and muffled giggles. Sometimes there was a look of disdain or contempt or righteous superiority. How she'd failed to deceive them into thinking her a widow, she couldn't guess, unless that was too common a ploy, used by many an unfortunate before her, too worn an excuse to take seriously.

However, if the looks wounded, the banter was usually whispered, did not confront her: they were, it seemed, not vindictive, these girls.

One hard-eyed woman, somewhat older, did take her aside one day to explain in a roundabout way that she did know of someone who could put paid to the whole episode. She would have a miscarriage and no-one would be the wiser. There was a price, of course. But all very cleanly and comfortably and quietly done.

Eliza, tempted for a moment, remembered the words of Sarah Hoskinson and declined the offer.

Sarah-Ann moved into No.34 Waugh Street with her husband and daughter. Diana was entranced by the baby and spent much time, when not at the spinning mill, at the house a few doors away, helping her sister, relaying stories of the baby's prowess to Eliza when she returned. Eliza tried to shut her ears to the prattle: she was still far from reconciled to the coming creature. Still, under Sarah Hoskinson's guidance she was building up a store of necessities. Sarah-Ann offered her her own baby's first bonnets, which she said Eliza-Ann was rapidly growing out of; and a shawl which was surplus to requirements, being a rather startling shade of red in an excessively loopy way of knitting.

For a cradle, the use of a drawer was recommended, well-padded with newspaper, rag and blanket. Put on the floor, a baby would not fall far even should it manage such a feat as getting out. Perhaps that was not altogether an advantage, thought Eliza, in a dark mood.

Sarah Hoskinson had taken Eliza to see the woman who would help her deliver. Eliza had gone, not wanting to, but was relieved to find the house clean, though poor and the woman unjudgmental and decent.

She still had not told their landlady, Mrs Booth. She waited for a Saturday evening when Mr Booth had gone out, as he did sometimes, to the pub on the corner. Then she went downstairs, finding Mrs Booth in the scullery, and asked if she could come upstairs for a moment or two. The children were left, with admonishments to 'mind the fire, now'.

Mrs Booth betrayed no surprise at the coming event. Indeed said that she had suspected something of the sort. But the two of them, Eliza and Diana, seemed respectable girls apart from that and they always paid their rent and on time too and not that she condoned it of course and the preachers did preach against it but then preachers were men weren't they and what did they know about such things and if asked she could tell Eliza a thing or two ... And on and on she burbled, like a chattering stream, while Eliza felt nothing but relief that they were not to be put out into the streets. For where they would go and what would happen to them then did not bear thinking about. The city abounded in drinking houses, gaudy and warm, through whose doors staggered wretched, tattered creatures, whose only means of surviving another day was to inveigle some man into paying for the use of their bodies.

It came to the end of September and the nights were drawing in. Eliza could still pass cursory scrutiny when shawled. Her brother-in-law came up with an idea.

'I've a mind to go to the theatre or such,' he said one Sunday. 'And Sarah-Ann, she wants to go an' all.'

'Oh, that'd be such a treat for her,' said Eliza. Then, with a spurt of generosity which astounded herself, 'Would you like me to mind the babby?'

'Nay, cariad. We thought to take you and Diana with us. Sister Anne says as she'll mind Eliza-Ann.'

'We've brought the *Courier* with us,' put in Sarah-Ann.

A Victorian Miss

The *Courier* came out both Wednesdays and Saturdays and they turned to its advertising section in hope.

'The *Royal*, they're doing *The Queen's Shilling* with *Old Cronies* coming afore it,' Sarah-Ann pointed out.

'Army things, likely,' said William. 'Sounds a bit of alright.'

Princes was showing Miss Ellen Terry in *The Merchant of Venice.* Of Ellen Terry they had all heard, but were somewhat dubious about sitting through the play she would appear in.

'Too high an' mighty for the likes of us,' ventured Sarah-Ann.

'Now, that's more the thing,' said William, pointing to the advertisement for the *Folly.* 'Arthur Roberts. He's made a name for himself, he has. Tours all the music hall circuits in the country. Used to go round to Evans's supper room in London after the performance like, and sing again, but much more saucy this time. Made a right stir. They've only just got their licence back, Evans's.' He chuckled appreciatively.

Eliza hesitated. Their father had never allowed his wife or girls to visit the music hall, though she suspected, from his habit of humming certain tunes, that he might not have obeyed his own instructions. What could be so bad about it? Anyway, Sarah-Ann was now a married woman; and if her own husband did not object, what could her father do? And she herself had been cast out and could surely sink no further into wickedness.

She felt defiant. 'Let's go,' she said. 'Next Saturday evening. Only, how much is it?'

'Gallery, 6d,' said William. 'That's the cheapest.'

Diana looked pleadingly at her older sister. The poor girl didn't have much amusement in her life, thought Eliza. What she did have was much hard work, all of which she performed uncomplainingly. Well, almost uncomplainingly.

'We shall afford it,' she announced.

Under the repetitive work at the mill that week lay a layer of joyous expectation. The days were lightened by thought of the treat to come; and the time of the performance drew excitingly ever nearer.

Much time was spent by each girl in wondering if she would look her best in the blue skirt or the brown. Would it be too showy to reveal a bracelet or brooch? Their choices were not too difficult to make, their range being so very limited. But hair could be changed: plaits wound around the head? Or hair smoothed into a neat bun behind? Or should that be bulked out to make more of a show? Or curls could fall onto a shoulder or over a forehead in wanton disarray. Perhaps not that, Eliza thought.

They could not keep their expedition to themselves: it bubbled out of them, so that various girls in the carding and spinning rooms were apprised of their coming adventure; and the talk started up of this comic and that, the most amusing ever seen. Others, they found, would also be going to the *Folly* that same night; and they promised to look out for each other and wave in recognition.

Chores were performed quickly that Saturday afternoon. Basins of warm water were carried up to their bedroom, skin soaped and dried, hair put into papers with prayers that the procedure would have time to 'take'. Clothes had been sponged and brushed, missing buttons resewn, petticoat lace firmly re-applied, boots shined.

At six they left Waugh Street together, feeling conspicuously well-dressed, making their way first south down Palmerston Street before turning west towards the city centre. In Peter Street, outside the *Folly*, they joined the queue which already snaked too far for comfort.

'What'll we do if we can't get in?' asked Diana, almost too afraid to refer to such a tragedy.

'Don't you fret, cariad,' said her brother-in-law comfortingly. 'We shall get in alright.'

And so they eventually would, but the slow shuffle of the queue as they waited their turn was barely to be born.

The sky dimmed and a lamplighter appeared in the distance, lighting the gas-lamps one by one with the long pole he carried. Eliza realized that soon, not only would they be climbing out of bed in the dark, as indeed they were already; but they would be leaving the mill in the dark besides.

She shivered at the thought of those frosty mornings, when ice-pictures would appear on the window overnight and clothes would have to be sandwiched between the covers, both for extra warmth at night and for comfort in the morning; and when trying to pull on undergarments without exposure to icy bedroom air would become a skill worth honing.

'You'll never guess.' William interrupted her thoughts. 'Young Alfred, he gave me a whole 6d piece, said to buy some refreshments with it. Not known for throwing money away, that one.' He shrugged.

'Ices,' said Diana, longingly.

A popular tune, played on harmonica, grew louder as they drew abreast. Eliza, feeling full of largesse, threw a half-penny into the hat and was rewarded by a nod and a glance of thanks. Then they were in the lobby, its warmth and its opulence of gold and cream and red. Photographs of the famous lined the walls. William bought their tickets and they became a part of the snake heading upwards.

They found themselves on high, 'Up in the clouds,' said Diana, settling herself with contentment; and the clouds already beginning to rise from pipe-smokers below and around enhanced the illusion. There was an expectant hum of chatter, discordant sounds as the musicians tuned up, and the odd burst of excited laughter as everyone settled into their seats.

Then the band struck up, the curtain rose and after some warm-up acts the star of the evening appeared. So handsome he was, so debonair, so extravagantly costumed. He carried his audience with him and they carried him. They roared with laughter. Sometimes Eliza looked sideways at her younger sister to find her laughing, but, Eliza assessed, laughing rather along with the audience than always having the full sense of the, often seamy, joke, an observation which soothed her slight guilt as to whether they should have brought her.

Songs were sung from the stage; and sometimes the audience joined in with enthusiasm; and they clattered out of the *Folly* holding a vision of a more joyful, carefree world.

'If only we could keep doing this sometimes,' declared Diana, 'life would be so much easier to be cheerful about.'

They hesitated near a brazier and the tantalising scent

of crisping potato skin; but hurried on. Sarah-Ann, she said, needed to get back to her firstborn, still largely reliant on her milk and who might by now, according to its mother, be screaming with all the power of its lungs and going positively blue in the face.

'The longer you feeds 'em, the less likely you are to start another,' she said to Eliza in a quiet aside. 'An' the longer that be, the better.'

'That was a truly splendid evening,' said Diana sleepily as they curled up in bed, close for the warmth.

Eliza stroked her sister's hair. 'You're a good girl,' she said.

There were few leaves to strew the cobbles of Ancoats to show the turn of the year. The mornings became a little mistier. And the ever-present smoke hung in the mist to thicken it and darken it, so that on some days, if you hadn't known every street and every turn of the way, you might have lost yourself between home and mill.

But then, reflected Eliza, you were carried in a stream, thin as a trickle at first, fed by tributaries on all sides, until the whole river swept through the mill gates. At the day's end the reverse happened, so that they poured out in a flood of jostling, clacking bodies, which siphoned off up side-channels, so that you reached your own street as two of a baker's dozen, fumbling along the walls, coughing from the fog that got in the chest.

As the days grew shorter, and of a late afternoon, just as heads had to be held closer to the job in hand and the feeling of irritation and complaint was growing among women, catching each other's eyes. turned them up to

Heaven in solidarity, a belated man came in to light the gas jets.

Though, on the one hand, the sudden light was a welcome relief to straining eyes and welcome also as a signal that home-time was drawing nearer; on the other hand, lighting the jets also brought a measure of trepidation.

The scavengers, at this point, were chivvied to sweep with care and without raising undue dust. For one of the great dangers that attended the production of cotton was fire. Cotton dust could create an explosive mixture in the air. And mills were packed full of cotton. In past times, when wooden boards and wooden beams had been used in their building, serious fires, sometimes total destruction, had been common. Nowadays, folk reassured themselves, a better method had been found: the fire-proof mill, where brick and iron reigned supreme.

Nevertheless, danger still lurked; and gas jets were a hazard. Fire illuminated the newspaper pages at least once a month; fire, if not in Manchester itself, in the mills, most usually the cotton-spinning-mills, of Woodley or Burnley or Oldham. Fire engines rushed to the scene and roofs fell fierily within. Few workers lost their lives, but there were narrow escapes, as in Rochdale that October, where 'many of the operatives lost a part of their clothing, and some their watches'. A particular trial indeed, reflected Eliza, somewhat puzzled.

In November, fire broke out in Ancoats itself, at nine o'clock in the morning, this time a silk mill, its first three storeys engulfed in flame, with spread into the engine-house and the cellar. The fire brigade brought a steam fire-engine, three tenders, a hand-worked engine and an escape; and within an hour had subdued the flames. This prompt defeat was attributed to the mill's fireproof qualities. And as the mill was well-insured, reasonable confidence was put in economic recovery.

On Saturdays and Sundays in particular, brass bands reigned supreme. To be a member of a band was to gather where a man could meet his friends, indulge himself with harmony, show loyalty to a tribe; and, hopefully, preen himself with success.

Competitions were rife, eagerly awaited, assiduously practised for and entered with high hopes: gold medals were a source of pride; and new instruments donated and won gave the band an edge over its competitors. Thus, more prizes.

Bands played in parks and they played in halls. They played at important events, like the laying of foundation stones, at the openings of canals, railways and roads and to celebrate anniversaries. An occasion would hardly be considered complete unless blessed and graced by the rousing strains of a brass band.

The police force had a band, the Reform School had a band, the Temperance Movement had a band, factories had bands, railway companies had bands. Music was all.

And as Christmas approached, that year of 1880, many music-lovers turned to the highlight of the season: Handel's Messiah. Manchester was in love with the Messiah. The two great rival performances were those conducted by Mr Edward De Jong and by Mr Charles Hallé respectively. Each boasted 350 members of band and choir. Each admitted commoners for a price of 1s.

Many other places, such as churches, even the

Cathedral, feeling perhaps inadequate to the magnitude of the complete task, put on selections.

But by the time the Messiah was drawing near, Eliza had neither heart nor strength for celebrations. Her body grew more and more heavy and she was so *tired.* Heaving herself out of bed in the mornings became a coupled effort of body and will. The work wore her out.

By the end of the day her body was an aching lump that she made perform by pure determination, conscious too that most accidents happened at this time of day, when operatives were too fatigued to stay alert to danger.

When home she wanted to do nothing but rest and sleep. The creature inside her battered to be released. Or so she thought of it.

And she worried. She had built up a store of coins, hidden, not beneath the mattress, but beneath a loose floorboard. Would it be enough to feed herself, and Diana through the period before she could work again? Would she even live, to work again? And, in one of her frequent changes of emotion, she found herself wretchedly fretting about what would happen to the baby, suppose it lived and she did not? She pleaded with Sarah-Ann, and Sarah-Ann promised to care for the baby if Eliza died, though she told her sister vehemently that this was a nonsense and all would be well. Then she was filled with apprehension of how, if both she and the baby survived, was she ever to care for it when she resumed work? This she tried to put off thinking about. Part of her hoped she would die and the baby too: it must be a fitting punishment for her sin.

Partway through the Monday afternoon of the 20th of

A Victorian Miss

December, and everyone in a bright mood looking forward to a full day off on the following Saturday, being Christmas Day, with Sunday a holiday anyway and the Monday one of the new Bank Holidays, Eliza felt a strange sensation in her belly. She carried on working. But again it came and a little afterwards, it happened a third time. She had already given the statutory notice, so called over the overlooker; and left the premises. Diana, finding her absent when the hooter boomed its mournful signal for the downing of tools, would surely have the nous to understand the situation. She made her way haltingly to the house of the woman who now must be either her saviour or her nemesis, where she was questioned and prodded and the contractions taken account of. Then she was put to bed.

A long and confused time of pain and terror followed where she lost all dignity and did not care.

Suddenly, release came. The pain was over, herself full of wonder and relief and the midwife holding to her a red and screwed-up face.

'It's a boy,' she said.

Eliza's first startled thought was that she didn't have a name for a boy. Babies came in the female gender. Her family did not produce boys.

Her second thought was one of hope. On the rare occasion that a boy baby had been born, it soon died. Then she gazed at the helpless, fragile piece of humanity. And, for the same reason, was swept by fear.

She caught at the tiny hand whose fingers latched around her own. And felt, without warning, a huge tide of love. She cradled the scrap of a thing and the midwife positioned it against her breast and Eliza was overwhelmed with the love, so much that it overflowed into a hiccupping sea of tears.

She stayed with the woman for a few days before going back to Waugh Street. Diana looked and marvelled. Sarah-Ann the same. With this sister, Eliza discussed an idea she'd had.

'Sarah-Ann,' she began, 'You're still feeding Eliza-Ann. And you don't have to go out to work.'

'That's right,' agreed her sister.

'Suppose,' said Eliza, 'I fed the baby in the evening and in the night and in the morning before I left for work, and I came back from the mill to feed him in the dinner-time. If you took care of him while I was at the mill and he got hungry, would you give him a little yourself? And I'd pay you,' she went on. 'It would help out all round.'

Sarah-Ann considered this for a long moment. 'I'd be proud to help you, sister,' she said. 'An' what's more, I'm writing to our dad.'

Eliza was taken aback.

'Well, it's a boy. A boy! You know how our father is about boys. Who knows but he might forgive you, with a real grandson of his own. Now, what are you going to call him?'

'I thought William,' said Eliza. 'After your husband as he's been so good to us. And after our mother's brother, the one who went to be a soldier, the one she was so fond of.'

'And he never married because of being in the army so he's got no children of his own? I shall write and tell him that he's to have a great-nephew named after him.'

A Victorian Miss

Eliza smiled; and after a moment Sarah-Ann went on, 'So you're not going to call him John then? After our dad? It might melt his stony heart. And he might take against you and the babby if you don't.'

'He will *not,* he will NOT, be called John.'

'You'll have to go and see the registrar soon as you can.'

'Yes,' said Eliza. She had given much thought to this over the last few days.

'Would you like me to come with you?'

'I think I'll be going on my own, but thank you all the same,' said Eliza.

Two weeks after the birth, and carrying the baby in a sling on her back, she visited a registry. It was not in Ancoats and she had some way to walk. It was the 5th of January. Within her raged the spirit of a she-wolf.

The clerk took a pinkish, red-lined form from a pile; and regarded her dourly over his spectacles.

'Date on which the child was born?'

'The 21st of December, 1880.'

'Address at which the child was born?'

'No.9, Percival Street.'

'Name of the child?'

'William Alfred Kirby.'

'Sex of child?'

'Boy.'

'Name of the child's father?'

'John Kirby.'

'Occupation of father?'

'Bricklayer.'

Name of mother?'

'Eliza Kirby.'

'Formerly?'

'Formerly Bladen.'

The document received a few embellishments, such as its registration district of Chorlton-upon-Medlock, today's date; and Eliza's confirming signature.

She left the office feeling fully satisfied. No, she had not been strictly truthful. But, 'Best not give too much away,' their father had always said. 'Them as is in authority'll allus get you if they can, out of sheer devilment. Dunna thee give 'em a chance, girl.'

And the certificate did hold a pinch of truth; and what was not truth did at least refer to known people and places.

No.9, Percival Street, though not at all the address where the child had actually been born, had been their family home for years before leaving for Birmingham. And it was a respectable address, its weekly rent 8s.6d.

Her mother's married name had been the same as her own. Maybe the father's name was a stretch too far - though John Kirby had always been and would always be, most truly and proudly, a bricklayer - but who would ever complain? At least both those names, John and Eliza, had lived together at 9, Percival Street.

Authority was satisfied. No-one but herself and Authority need see the child's second name, and Authority would not be interested. The reason for the child's second name, Alfred, was her secret; and perhaps sometime in the future, the child would learn its significance.

Most importantly, armed with that document, no-one could accuse her child of being a bastard.

A Victorian Miss

5
1881
BONDS, BATHS AND BONHOMIE

Time became blurred, a waste of tiredness. Will was a hungry baby and he fed often. Not for him the four-hourly pattern Eliza had envisioned, the tidy feed followed by the swift mop-up and change of rag.

She removed the rag now. It was dirtied and this time she would throw it away: the earth closet would swallow it. She thought of her rag-store and wondered whether it would last out. Probably she would need more. The square that was pinned outside the rag was wet, but would have to do again. She hung it to dry on the rope that criss-crossed the room. It was impossible to properly wash and dry each change of nappy.

Sarah-Ann had told her to catch Will just before he dirtied his nappy and hold him over a chamber-pot. Made life simpler, she said. Sometimes Eliza succeeded in this, but not today. The room stank of faeces and urine from drying nappies, with an underlay of sour milk from the baby-clothes, even though she had him in a cotton bib which caught most of the dribble and was easier to wash. Everyone bar the rich wore something to protect their clothes: the rich had the poor to wash for them and had no need to save on work.

Eliza dreamed for a short while of being rich, of reclining elegantly along a sofa, listening to a sister play a soft air on a piano; and stretching out a languid hand to ring a bell for a maid to appear with a tray of tea and buttered crumpets. She watched the maid retire with an, 'Anything further, Ma'am?' and a curtsey, before coming back to the top front in Waugh Street. At least it was Sunday.

Later that day they were due to go to Sarah Hoskinson's house in Palmerston Street. It was a good house, with, at the front, beyond the pleasure of a little hall, a well-kept parlour for events and vicars, not that Sarah had much occasion for either; but it was a solace to know that such a room was there if ever needed in that capacity.

Behind was a comfortable kitchen, with a large iron range, hob above and oven by the side, where all the cheerful, everyday life of the house went on. And behind again, covering one half of the width, was a scullery, quite roomy, with water that ran from an inside tap. Mr Hoskinson, who was a practical sort of a man, in touch with a phalanx of other practical men and the latest inventions, and besides was very fond of his pretty young wife, had arranged for a feature of sheer luxury here. For besides the cold tap there was another; and the water that issued from this could be made hot, by means of a long, coiled water-pipe heated by gas jets.

So that when Mr Hoskinson returned, gritty and scratchy from a long day of brick-manufacture or the over-seeing of, he could strip off in the scullery and, sitting in a zinc bath, soap and rinse himself to his heart's content in hot water.

Whilst his wife, of a Monday, could wash clothes in a zinc barrel, made expressly for the purpose, renewing the hot water with fresh as often as she saw fit. Eliza could feel only envy.

Will had been fed before daylight, fed at 9.30, fed at 1.30, for once delightfully obedient to a four-hourly rhythm. He had been changed, wrapped and bonneted against the cold; and finally swathed in Eliza's shawl before being slung onto her back. Diana darted hither and thither, fetching and handing, amusing Will with snatches of song and cooing noises. Eliza looked at her with affection.

Outside, it was an ice-grey day; the sky above was a heavy, strangely thick, one-tone grey; the townscape in various tones from paler to darker, but grey, a grey relieved only by a dim redness of brick behind its coat of soot. Though when was Ancoats other than grey? It was as if it had been left half-finished, no-one bothering to paint it.

They walked the short distance to No.148, and as they left the house, specks began to fall, white and delicate as they floated to earth, the few becoming a multitude, a whirling mass that feathered out harsh edges, brought a soft whiteness to the world. Crystals fell icy on a stuck-out tongue. The girls laughed, hurrying on, eyes half-shut against the teeming flakes.

Then, a knock on the door, a wave of warm air, a de-shawling, a whisking away of wet garments including Will's outer baby-shawl and bonnet, followed by an ushering into, of all sacred places, the front parlour, where a coal fire was throwing out a glorious heat, interrupted only by the person of Joseph, standing legs wide before it, thumbs in his waistcoat pockets.

Greetings were exchanged, Joseph's cheery enquiry as to the health of his erstwhile friend John Kirby meeting with a regretful shake of the head. He peered at Will with a few hmmms expressive of approbation or at least acceptance. His wife called him an old curmudgeon, though in such an affectionate way that no-one suspected her of meaning it, and they settled themselves round the piano.

A piano could live in no place other than a grand front parlour. Sarah hardly played, having grown up in a tiny village in the country somewhere, where most people probably worked the land and were unable to afford such luxuries as pianos. Eliza, however, could play. Their father had followed his desire for respectability by insisting that his daughters learn to play the piano. Girls they were, and as such necessarily disappointing, but they would be trimmed into specimens of the breed as superior as he could make them. At 9 Percival Street they had owned a very respectable piano.

It was not Eliza though who excelled, nor the absent Sarah-Ann, but the youngest of the three, Diana. She took her seat with shy grace, Eliza at hand to turn the score.

A Victorian Miss

They began with, by request, *Early One Morning,* progressing through *Oh Dear, What Can the Matter Be?*

After a while came *Champagne Charlie,* which Joseph enlivened by taking his hat and a stick from the hall and striding outrageously up and down the room pouring non-existent champagne into a tall glass, while singing loudly in his not-always-quite-on-key baritone. That spurred him on to request *The Girl I Left Behind Me,* 'In honour of yer father, who was a hero, tha knows.'

This, Eliza and Diana were well aware of, their father and their mother both having numerous times recounted the tale of John Kirby's going to war, not to fight, but to near single-handedly build a railway which saved the mighty British Army from defeat in the Crimean War. The girl he'd left behind him had been of course their mother. John Kirby's idea of himself as hero had possibly been one of the strands that led, Eliza thought, to his rejection of her and the baby: she had tarnished the cherished image.

Eliza retreated from the company to give the beginning-to-grizzle Will his next feed, while she from a plate by her side, and the rest of the gathering round the table, ate Sarah's buttery muffins and fruit cake. Joseph Hoskinson was doing well at his trade.

Sarah-Ann had acted on her own suggestion and had written to their father soon after Will's birth, informing him that he had a thriving grandson. The letter had been directed to Birmingham, using the address where they had been lodging. So far there had been no reply. Eliza wondered if there ever would be. Would he ever forgive?

Someone pulled back the curtain to reveal a few more

snowflakes fluttering down; and Sarah was spurred to tell them of life as a girl in her country village where they skated in the icy weather, or rather, slid about on the ice where streams had overflowed and frozen. She remembered, she said, seeing the young gentry skating fast over a lake, wearing special, metal-bladed boots.

Prince Albert, Joseph put in reminiscently, had liked to skate; almost drowned once, in the lake at Buckingham Palace, romantically saved from death by his young wife.

Eliza imagined Will, grown tall and limber, swooping across the ice in a lace-white stillness. Her vision was so very unlike Ancoats.

The sing-song resumed. A few hymns were sung to honour the day, then the mournful *Barbara Allen*, the romantic *Drink to Me Only with Thine Eyes*; and the *Drunken Sailor* with much improvisation, largely by Joseph; and which made them laugh till they woke up Will. The finale was *Home! Sweet Home!*

Joseph gallantly saw them back to Waugh Street. The snow had stopped its faery falling and was, in places, already being trampled to a slithery, slushy blackness, which glinted in the occasional light from such windows as were curtainless and the gleam of Joseph's lantern. It was cold, cheerless and ominous, as if unknown things might be lurking: Eliza was glad of Joseph's male sturdiness.

Life went on. Life was a rush; constant, unrelenting. It was a trial to prise oneself from one's bed into shrinking cold, a rush to feed Will, a scramble to change and pacify him, a rush to Sarah-Ann's house to hand him over with a pang, a rush to reach the mill on time so as not to incur a fine, a rush to deal with all the work that was demanded on time, before time, however fast you thought you'd worked. The dinner hour was no respite, hurrying to get to her sister's house, to feed Will, to feed herself. Then more work and the rush home to feed Will again.

'The other lasses've been talking,' said Diana, one morning. The sun had lit up their room and the napkins drying across the room smelt worse than ever.

'Some of them go to the New Islington Baths in Ancoats. There's a laundry there with washing troughs and drying stoves, wringers and mangles as well. And you can have a warm bath with a towel and soap. And there's a swimming bath for ladies as well as the ones for the men. There wasn't one to start with but the ladies pressed so hard that the City Council had to put one in.'

Eliza took in this information. In all her life she had never used a fixed bath with taps where the water just ran in as you wished: houses with a rent below £21 a year were not allowed to install these, unless they paid a special charge, that is. And who could do that? The house in Percival Street would have just qualified for the dignity of a bath, but the landlord must have thought it unnecessary.

She vaguely remembered some Public Baths being opened just before their father had dragged them all off to Birmingham, something too about cleanliness being next to godliness and the importance of being clean because it kept you healthy. She imagined being able to properly wash all Will's clothes and all their clothes too. It would be almost as good as buying new. She imagined lying in glorious hot water and cleansing every part of her body. It sounded bliss beyond words.

'When's it open?'

'They say every day. Sundays just from six till eight in the morning, because of Church of course. And then Tuesdays and Thursdays the swimming's for the better classes and it costs more - sixpence. For us on other days it'd be tuppence. Then there's wash-baths an' a wash-house.'

'We s'll have to find the money,' Eliza said firmly. 'For the washing, I mean.'

And they did, rising earlier than usual on a Sunday and walking to New Islington which turned out to be only a few streets away. The houses here were gimcrack, mostly one-up-and-one-down; and tightly packed each was too. Children, already up and out, shoeless and ragged, played on pavements and splashed in gutters.

How many of them would grow into adults? Eliza felt apprehensive as she looked from them to her precious Will: children's lives were precarious in Manchester.

'Do you remember, Diana,' she said suddenly, 'our dad being a Socialist?'

'He used to go on about how they wanted better lives for people like us,' said Diana.

'He said we ought to have a share in all that wealth the bosses took for themselves. Said people like him did all the work and the bosses got the rewards. Not a lot's changed, has it?'

They looked around them, at the mean houses, the ragged children.

'Still, he said things had all been worse when he was a

boy, 'specially in places like Manchester he said, places that were growing quickly. Streets filled with piles of stinking rubbish, or pools of stinking offal. One, two families living all together in a cellar, sleeping on straw, no beds or anything. And the floor running with water or stuff from cesspits.' She pulled a face.

'And the pigs,' said Diana with relish, transferring her bundle of washing from one shoulder to the other. 'I do so remember the pigs. They slept in the cellar as well, until they got eaten by the people. And in the day they lived off horrible things, rooting around in the streets, in those awful piles and pools.'

'And one dunny for a hundred people,' said Eliza.

'There's still lots that have to share dunnies,' said Diana. 'And you told me about that bit in the paper, remember? Said that fourteen and a half thousand houses in Manchester, this very year, *now*, haven't got running water inside the house.'

'Like these here, I'd think,' said Eliza, looking at them with a jaundiced eye.

Not everyone agreed with the Socialists, she knew. There were plenty of minds set against them. Trouble was, the minds mostly belonged to the people that mattered, the ones that spoke loudly from pulpits and in Parliament. Socialists, they said - and they got very cross about it - were against all marriage, all private property and all religion. They were wicked people and they would destroy our precious country.

The Socialists still weren't in charge, mused Eliza, but perhaps they'd nudged the law into bettering things a bit. There wasn't that much filth in modern streets. Builders had new, stricter rules to obey. Cellars weren't these days

- or at least they weren't supposed to be - used as your only home.

Of the other things that had been, still were, complained about, you did even today see folk with missing bits, and heard of families driven into the workhouse because the breadwinner had been killed in an accident at work. There had been a case not long since, where a man had had the flesh burnt from an arm trapped between revolving drum and beam; and another where the hair and its scalp had been torn off; and in neither case had their employers had to part with any money to help them at all.

Although there had been something recently, about a worker being able to sue the boss if he'd been injured in an accident at work. But he had to prove it was the boss's fault. There the bosses held all the cards, Eliza thought: the gift of the gab, the money to hire a lawyer, being on dining terms with the local magistrate. It was a worthy idea, one of those kindly Christian ones, well, Socialist ones perhaps; but she didn't think the worker stood much of a chance.

'Expect Father's still going on about it all,' she said to Diana. 'But to Mrs Ward these days.'

They had brought with them all their own and Will's dirty garments and it was a joy to see them come clean again. Then Diana had a bath whilst Eliza, hindered by Will, saw to the mangling and drying before roles were exchanged. Will, after an initial and noisy fright, had a sudden change of mind, and gave himself fully to the exploitation of the magical substance.

They emerged feeling more clean than they had

thought possible. And it was a wonder beyond words to possess a stock of clothes not only clean, but already near to dry.

'We shall come again,' Eliza said; and Diana smiled with satisfaction.

Life went on in its humdrum way through March and into April. Then there came a Bank Holiday. This one was Easter Monday, which in the year of 1881 fell on the 18th of April. These annual days of glory, sometimes called St Lubbock's Days after the man who had persuaded Parliament of the benefits of his Good Idea, had been instituted ten years previously. Workers had four whole new days of rest throughout the year, to add to Good Friday and Christmas Day which had been holidays from time immemorial.

Another much-prized holiday which was gradually taking hold was Wakes Week. This had hazy religious roots to sanctify it, but was becoming useful to the mill-owners. Mill machinery could not work perpetually at its best without being oiled and sharpened, checked for wear, new components replaced for old, occasionally the latest model installed. It was proving economical to shut the whole mill down for this and pay skilled men to do the repair work, with all machinery at rest, rather than do a bit here and a bit there through the year

The major part of the work-force could have a holiday and bless their beneficent employer at the same time. They were not paid, of course, but an employer, or a union, could set up a club to save precious pence to see them through the week.

Wakes Weeks had been held the previous year in

Oldham, in Stoke, in Longsight, Matlock, Rochdale and other places near, though not in Manchester as such. Wakes Week, however, if it might come at all, would be way ahead. For the Easter Monday they decided on Belle Vue. They had all, except Will and little Eliza-Ann, visited before: it was a popular outing. Food for the adults they would take with them: for the small ones it would be naturally available.

The day dawned bright and clear, but Diana, issuing early on a visit to the privy, reported a biting wind: a nuisance, but not unexpected at Easter. They would wrap up well.

They walked into Piccadilly in the city centre and stood in a queue. Trams no sooner arrived than they were filled with eager passengers and they were quickly on their way. The ride was an expense but needful; and quite an excitement besides, for they had climbed to the upper deck, to view the city spread out, something you couldn't easily appreciate when walking at ground level.

Descending, they had to wait for only a short while until the Gardens opened at 10am, by which time the snake of sightseers had trebled in length, paying their sixpences as they passed the gatekeeper with his leather bag.

Inside was vast, but there were maps to show you where to go. The animals were the major attraction and the party made towards them through the gardens. Flowers were blooming, though no-one was very sure as to their names. Tulips were recognised and commented on; and there were some trees festooned in blossom of whites and pinks. This was something never seen in the brick-bare streets of Ancoats.

A strange feeling crept into Eliza. She saw green shoots pushing upwards and outwards, flowers opening into delicate beauty: there came a waking sense of alertness, of promise, not only for the growing things, but an unfurling springing from inside herself. Perhaps her life was not ended. Perhaps there was a future beyond the drear present.

'Look you, over there now, there's an elephant!' said William proudly, as if he had discovered the species. Eliza-Ann, ten months old now, waved at the vast creature. Will was asleep, flopped over Eliza's back. Sarah and Joseph's two boys were entranced.

They moved on to the lions, which woke Will up and made him cry. Eliza-Ann shouted back and the lions, who had cold, yellow eyes, waved their tails with bobbles on the end. There were tigers with stripes, pacing up and down, up and down; and cumbersome hippos; and rhinos with thick folds of leather coat and impressive horns, one behind the other. Sarah's boys stared, drinking in their strangeness. Some people threw buns to them. 'Wasteful,' said Eliza, crossly.

At dinner-time they tried to shelter from the wind in the lee of a wall and munched their hunks of bread and jam.

They were overlooking a lake and as they watched, a charming little steamer began to take passengers on board. Diana's eyes grew large and she breathed a sigh of longing. The boys sat up, pointing out to each other all they knew about boats; which did not amount to a great deal.

'How much to go on the steamer?' asked Joseph.

'I'll go, bach, have a look at that board over there,' said William, rising to his feet. He came back at a trot. 'One penny for each of us,' he said. 'But the babbies can go free. Not the boys. They'll have to pay, see.'

Joseph felt in his pockets. 'Try what I've got in 'ere.'

He drew out a fistful of coins, counting the company the while. 'Eight. Eight pence it is.'

The meal finished and the babies fed, they made their way down to the pier. One boat was unloading passengers, another half-way through its journey round the lake. Soon they were stepping uncertainly aboard, Diana keeping close to Eliza and gazing lakeward, the boys edging up to everything of interest, such as the cabin from which the boat was steered.

'See she's called the Little Britain?' said Joseph. 'That's after the Great Britain, first iron steamship to cross the Atlantic to America. Isambard Kingdom Brunel, that was.'

'Famous engineer, built railways too,' put in William, as if they didn't know.

They passed the other steamer and, on each boat, all the passengers waved, even little Eliza-Ann, though Will hadn't mastered the art as yet.

'That's the Little Eastern,' said Joseph. 'A penny if you lads can tell me about the Great Eastern.'

There was a silence. Then, 'Was it a ship?' ventured John, the elder.

'She, yer calls ships 'she',' reproved his father. 'You'm right. She were a ship. Biggest ship ever built. So big couldn't launch 'er. Took 'em months. Then she kept 'avin' accidents.'

'Glad we're on this boat, then,' said Sarah-Ann, with a mock shiver.

Came May and June; and Will was now six months old and was growing and cooing and had not been ill like most babies and was, thought Eliza, the most beautiful baby there had ever been. But she worried for him in the winters of the future that would come accompanied by the fogs of Ancoats. Not that winter was in the least close as yet: the weather had plentiful days of sun and heat. Though they made little difference to the cheer of the place, for the background of unrelenting hardness and angularity and dinginess never changed. Washing put out of doors to dry became sprinkled with smuts. Windows grew a film of grime.

Eliza saved and Diana saved, but it was not enough to make for themselves a better life.

June 6th was another Bank Holiday, the previous day having been Whit Sunday. Whit, with a few days off, was the nearest that canny Manchester mill-owners had as yet come to a Wakes Week.

Joseph took his family to Belle Vue again, not so much for the gardens as for the outdoor representation of a scene featuring the bay and town of Navarino. At night there was a re-enactment of the Battle half-a-century gone, where English, French and Russians had had a glorious victory over Turks and Egyptians. There were hand-to-hand encounters, ships on fire, mighty explosions. The boys ran about violently bang-banging each other and friends for weeks afterwards.

Eliza had feared the effect of sudden loud noises on her son; and she and Diana had joined the crowds of incomers who thronged into Manchester to gawp. They made for the School of Art where they looked at paintings, embroidery, Indian silks, Japanese work, gold and silver, china and glass, and all for 6d. Will, while seemingly content with the care and attention he was being given, made few noises of appreciation of the artistry, though his mother and aunt admired many wondrous, bedazzling things.

His brother Alfred, William told everyone, had gone with the Lancashire Artillery Volunteers to their annual camp. Eliza visualised tents and the sea, camp fires and camaraderie; and was deeply covetous of his good fortune. His brother Alfred, said William, was becoming known as something of a lad, a bit on the wild side. Eliza thought wryly that that had been going on longer than William was aware of; and she suspected that William, so solidly domesticated, was envious.

William himself dragged his somewhat unwilling wife to a day of bicycle racing.

'Look you, look at the prizes, cariad. You can win big money at the bicycle racing - £20 - all for riding faster than the next man. Have to have a bike first, mind. One day I shall buy one. When I'm rich, like.'

Sarah-Ann said nothing. Baby Eliza-Ann enjoyed the day, even though she once had to be rescued when, without warning, she scurried off on all fours, heading out into the path of a bunch of unsuspecting riders. Her parents were far more upset than she was.

It was in September when Sarah-Ann received a letter,

a letter that she had long given up hoping for. It was from their father. He was married, he said. He thought they should know. His new wife was Emily, Mrs Ward. He did not explain who Mrs Ward was, but that they knew: she was the monthly nurse who had been so helpful to Sarah-Ann in her confinement, the fortunate mother of many sons.

'He says they married in Burton-on-Trent,' said Sarah-Ann, puzzled. 'What would they want to go all that way for?'

'Maybe it's a delightful place for a honeymoon,' said Eliza. 'With all that beer.' And after a while, 'Or maybe no-one was there to know them.'

'Whatever happened to Mr Ward?' mused Sarah-Ann. But that they were never to discover.

6
1882
CATASTROPHE

Spring, summer, came and passed. Another autumn gloomed over Ancoats. Christmas came, with the Day itself falling on a Sunday. The mill closed as usual at one o' clock on the Saturday, Christmas Eve. Eliza waited at the gate for Diana to join her and they set off on the familiar route home.

It was quiet, as it always was when the machinery ceased to whirr and pound and clatter. Machines dominated the town. Manchester, chosen in part for its dampness, was Cottonopolis, the place where Cotton was King, ruling the lives of its multitude of subjects.

It was cold too, as was usual when they left the steamy warmth of the mill's interior, but very cold today and icy; and both girls tightened their shawls around them.

Diana was greasing her fingers as they walked. She had recently been upgraded to piecer, a job which meant being always alert, running from place to place, looking for broken threads, then twisting the broken ends together between thumb and forefinger. Both were raw and painful. She kept a small packet of grease to soothe them when she could.

'I might've changed jobs,' she said, glumly, 'but the overlooker's the same.'

'The sharp-faced chap?' asked Eliza, alert.

'Him with the gingery whiskers and the nasty beady eyes,' confirmed her sister.

'And?' asked Eliza.

'Ada says to keep away. If you can. He tells girls to stay behind sometimes. They don't like him, none of them do. He's spiteful if you don't do what he wants.'

Eliza was silent, thinking. An overlooker had power, could sack a girl if he wished: his word against hers.

She sighed. 'Best keep clear of him,' she said. 'Stick with the other girls. Make out you didn't hear him if he calls you back.'

They walked on, leaving the mill and work behind, thoughts gradually turning in other directions.

Will was never absent from Eliza's mind for long. He was a year old now. He was pulling himself up on the furniture and she was sure he was about to take his first steps. She desperately hoped it would be when he was in her care and not that of Sarah-Ann.

She was breast-feeding him more rarely now, and Sarah-Ann breast-fed him not at all. Sarah-Ann's daughter was feeding entirely on bread-and-milk, mashed potato, mashed anything really and Will was doing almost the same. It was becoming easier to care for Will nowadays, his mother thought. She no longer had to drag herself from sleep during the nights, for instance.

Money came into her head: the anxiety of it was never far from the surface. She and Diana earned just enough to support the three of them, with an occasional, saved-for, treat. Occasionally Alfred slipped a coin or two into her hand. They were lucky, she supposed, luckier than many who begged in the streets or turned to prostitution or, when they could tolerate being starved no longer, had to go into the workhouse. Diana's slight rise in wages, as a piecer, was handy, but they still lived on a knife edge.

So many things could go wrong in life, so many sharp rocks and quicksands lay in wait, even when you were young and well and had the energy to work. But she must not think of bad things: it would bring ill-luck, her mother used to say, as if bad things would be attracted to you, lured by your thoughts of them.

There was a converse in this too: no sooner had you said, admiringly, of some implement or garment, 'By gum, this's lasted well,' than it would unaccountably break or develop a hole. So it was not wise to feel too secure in your luck either. At least, it was wise not to boast of it.

Will was collected and taken home. He was almost, almost walking, said Sarah-Ann.

'What'll us do this afternoon, then?' Eliza asked Diana, having shaken off her gloomy ponderings. They pored over the attractions advertised in the Courier.

'Be lovely to go skating at Pomona,' said Diana, longingly. 'Leastways go to watch.' Eight acres of grass had been flooded to a depth of six inches and this had now become a sheet of ice. Skaters would come from far and near.

'I think Will'd like that giant Christmas tree in Bridge Street better,' said his mother. 'And then we could go on to Lewis's. We'd not have to pay and we'd maybe be able to buy something as a Christmas treat, for the children anyway.'

Lewis's, a large establishment in Market Street, had been open for nearly two years now, selling initially everything a boy or a gentleman could possibly need for the person, beginning at the lower end with boots, rising through youths' football costumes, and aspiring as high as umbrellas. It was, though, beginning to widen its appeal, into tea, coffee, drugs and rugs; and its Christmas advertisement leapt off the page with promises of 'Electric Light', 'Enchanted Palace', 'Grand Christmas Carnival', 'Beautiful Show', a shop which would 'save the people one-fourth in all they buy'. Its pleasures pulled like a magnet. Equally compelling were the rumours: the brilliance of the electric light had caused over a hundred horses to bolt; its brightness had impaired the sight of several people. Dared they go?

They did; Will either on Eliza's back or carried sideways on her hip. He was becoming heavy now to transport any distance: she was relieved when Diana offered to take him for a while.

Will stared at the Christmas tree without expressing an opinion. He could say 'Mam a mam a mam' now, a delight to Eliza's heart, but was not yet very good at 'Auntie Diana'.

The electric lights they approached warily, for fear of

Will's eyes. Paying mind to their own, they felt no discomfort and so proceeded into the emporium amidst its Christmas extravagances. A new, and larger, frock for Will stretched their finances, but he did so need one, and they could not resist; and besides, they had been promised that it had saved them one-fourth the cost of what they would pay elsewhere.

The market, to which they went later, gas lit only but decorated with evergreens in swags and wreaths, the stallholders in festive mood, was thronged with families shopping for delicacies. They bought a bag of oranges and a selection of sugared pigs in pink, and sugared mice in white, to be shared amongst the children and sweet-toothed adults.

Dinner on Christmas Day was to be a communal affair at the parental George house in Ardwick, so that they bought sausages and mince pies to add to the cheer: a feast was more affordable if everyone contributed. Indeed, it could hardly be held without.

On Christmas Day morning they met up with William, Sarah-Ann and the eighteen-month-old Eliza-Ann and together they walked the half-mile or so to Ardwick and the house in Swindell's Buildings. It would have been good to have gone to the Cathedral they agreed, preferably in the afternoon when there would be a service of carols and excerpts from the Messiah, but there didn't seem time to fit everything in.

Eliza, looking at her sister, thought she observed something different about her, a thickening of the waist. Sarah-Ann caught her gaze.

'I was going to tell everyone today,' she said, colouring. 'But I see you've guessed. I'm in the family way again. And just as I've finished with that one.' She nodded towards her daughter, happily holding her father's hand. She did not look pleased.

'How far gone are you?' her sister asked.

'Three months, I think. I'm such a size, far bigger than when I was having her.'

'Probably because it's the second,' said Eliza. Sarah-Ann nodded. She looked unhappy and Eliza asked nothing more.

Dinner was a grand occasion. Much had been expended on the purchase of a piece of pork, which had been anxiously tended half the morning by Mrs George and her daughters. There were potatoes, both boiled and roasted, alongside the meat, together with onions, carrots and turnips. All was topped on the plate with gravy made from the drippings. Good beer stood alongside. Afterwards, a plum pudding, that had been simmering quietly on top of the range, was unwrapped from its cloth, cut into a dozen pieces and distributed amongst the company. The only person who did not enjoy the pudding was Will who, given a taste, pulled a face, gave a cry and, to everyone's vast amusement, spat it out.

To Eliza's relief, Alfred was missing. She had come to regard him as a good-natured youth, but a youth all the same, an embarrassing, overgrown sort of a youth and was glad he'd chosen to be with his Volunteers.

Toasts were drunk, gossip flowed, William and Sarah-Ann revealed their secret to the smiles and congratulations of the company. The women roused themselves to wash the dishes while some of the gathering fell into slumber. Carols began to be sung: *Once in Royal David's City, See Amid the Winter's Snow, O Little Town of Bethlehem.* Games were played: *Blind Man's Buff, Pin the Tail on the Donkey, Spin the Platter.*

Collapse came again. Suddenly Sarah-Ann began to rummage through her reticule.

'I almost forgot,' she said. She pulled out a letter.

'It's from Father,' she said; and read it out. John Kirby, with his new wife and her children, had moved to Aston. Their new address was 56 Carlyle Street. Business was good, with Emily's son Frank helping him. He enclosed a gift for his grandson. That was all.

'And look at it!' said Sarah-Ann, waving something aloft: it was a banknote, for a whole pound. She passed it over to Eliza, who took it wonderingly, thinking of all the things it could buy.

'Nothing for you, then?' she asked.

'Nothing,' said her sister flatly. '"Cept his good wishes.'

'Can't complain then,' said Eliza. 'You didn't even have those when we left him in Birmingham.'

'Mebbe it's the new wife,' said Mr George. 'Good influence.'

Diana nudged Eliza. 'Look there,' she said quietly. Eliza followed her pointing finger. Will had pulled himself up with the help of a chair. He turned round to face them, holding with one hand. A moment of steadiness on two feet and he took a step forward, then another and a third. And abruptly sat down. Everyone cheered and Eliza rushed to pick him up and hug him.

A Victorian Miss

'Best Christmas present I've ever had,' she said, half-laughing, half-crying with pride.

Work began again on the 27th of December, the mill-hands arriving bleary-eyed and grumpy at having to begin work again, at having to drag themselves from bed in the dark, at clattering in to gaslight and cotton-fluff, at performing the same task hour after hour. Still, in breaks they chattered and chaffed each other. Eliza had never grown particularly close to any of the other girls, but she was accepted now as one of them and could exchange news or banter with the rest. She could even lip-read a little, as the old hands did, against the clamour of the machines. She felt at home in the mill now. She supposed, bleakly, that it might well be home for the rest of her life.

The year 1882 dawned fine and bright. New Year's Day, another holiday: what bliss. Eliza and Diana were up rather later than usual, reluctant to stir, but their rising had at last been made imperative by Will who had climbed out of his drawer and was staggering around the little space there was in the bedroom. When he caught sight of a stray hairpin and began to convey it to his mouth, Eliza leapt from her bed.

They would not go to the races, nor to one of the several pantomimes which they deemed Will to be not yet capable of appreciating; and moreover, too expensive. Instead, they would join the crowds in the streets, which activity was free; and visit the New Year's Fair at Great St. James' Hall in Oxford Street to witness magic, marionettes and midgets, waxworks and wonders; which cost sixpence.

On the way they made resolutions, Diana's to be wise and good through the year to come. For, as she pointed out, 'We can't none of us tell what'll happen in 1882 and we must needs make the best of it.'

And then there did come a happening, one of those happenings that nobody could have foretold. It came in the shape of Sarah Hoskinson, unusually waiting in the slush of February for Eliza as she finished work at the mill one dark Wednesday evening.

'Sarah,' she said, startled. 'What're you here for? What's the matter?' For the normally calm and cheerful Sarah was looking anxious.

"Ast seen Joseph? 'Ast seen 'im at all?'

'Joseph? No. Why would I? What's amiss?' Eliza began to be alarmed. She took her friend's arm. 'Wait. We've to wait for Diana. She's always last on account of her having to come along all those passages. Tell me. What's going on?'

Sarah was almost weeping. 'It's Joseph. 'E's disappeared. 'E 'asn't come 'ome.'

'Not come home?' Eliza repeated. 'What do you mean, not come home? Since when?'

'Since Sat'day dinner-time. I waited and there was his dinner and it got cold and the boys kept asking and I thought ... well, I don't know as what I thought. But 'e never come 'ome all day and then in't morning 'e still weren't there. So I went and asked one of his workmates and 'e never turned up on the Sat'day at work at all. And they'd thought mebbe 'e was ill. And I didn't know what to tell 'em, but I did say 'e weren't ill, or he weren't ill on Sat'day morning and that wer't last time I saw 'im. Oh,

Eliza, what'll I do?' And she burst into sobs.

Diana came up then and looked from one to another.

'Sarah's all sixes an' sevens,' said Eliza. 'Joseph seems to've disappeared. But a man can't really disappear, can he? He must be somewhere ... Did he seem bothered at all?' This last to Sarah.

'Not as I noticed. 'E seemed 'is usual self.'

Eliza for a few moments was lost for ideas. Then, 'Did he leave a note? Have you looked?'

Sarah brightened, 'I 'aven't looked.' Then she relapsed again. 'But I'd've found it, wouldn't I? 'E'd've left it where I'd notice, like on't mantelpiece? And surely 'e wouldna go off and just leave a note? 'E'd a told me.'

Eliza was thinking. 'Someone's got to collect Will. Diana, could you go and fetch him and give him his tea? I'll go back with Sarah, help her look and we'll see if we can come up with any ideas. Don't fret, love. He's maybe at home this minute, waiting for you and getting himself all worried.'

Diana nodded and hurried off to Waugh Street, while the two friends set off back to Palmerston.

'The boys are in from school,' said Sarah. 'They keeps asking and I dunno what to tell 'em. I've just said 'e's gone away but 'e'll be back. 'E will be back, won't he?'

'What about his other children? Could something've happened to one o' them, do you think?'

'There's so many. And I don't know where they all are. And 'e'd a told me, surely.' Joseph had been a widower when he married Sarah and had half-a-dozen boys out in the world.

'He's bound to get in touch. He won't just leave you

like that, all on a sudden. Why?'

They had reached No.148. Sarah let herself in and her two boys came out of the back room. They looked up at their mother.

'Where's Dad? Hast found 'im?' asked the youngest, Jesse.

Sarah shook her head. 'But we will, me duck, don't you fret. Look, Auntie Eliza's come to 'elp us.'

Together the two women looked in all the places they could think of, but no note surfaced.

They looked among his clothes, but Sarah said that nothing but what he was wearing that fatal Saturday morning was missing.

'He'll come back,' said Eliza flatly. Then thought and asked, 'What about money?'

'Well, 'e keeps some for 'isself, but this week no more'n usual; and then there's some goes in a pot on't mantel for the burial man and such. And another for 'olidays or off sick. There's a fair bit there.'

'And is it still there?' Eliza asked. 'Has he taken any of it?'

Sarah tipped the coins out of the pots and counted. ''E's tekken nowt,' she said flatly.

The two women looked at each other.

''E paid the rent, paid up for the first quarter. That I do know. Why would 'e do that if 'e wanted rid of us? So that'll do us for another month. But then what'll we do? If he don't come back? I couldna pay for this house, not wi' working at mill and that's the only work I'd get. An't boys aren't old enough to work, only six and five.'

Eliza consoled as best she could; but that her friend was likely worrying for nothing was topmost in her mind, and was what she said. By now it was getting late: with the early start to work the next day, she had to get home.

'Sarah, I'm that sorry, Sarah. I don't want, I really don't want, to leave you like this, but I'm going to have to go. I'll think all I can. An' you too. And we'll pray that he comes back soon.'

The awful spectre of an accident flashed across Eliza's mind, but Sarah didn't seem to have yet considered that, so she said nothing. Anyway, if Joseph had had an accident, wouldn't someone have come by now with the news?

'I'll come here and see you tomorrow after work,' she said. 'By then, you'll be wondering why you worried.'

But as she made her way home, she found herself not believing in her own words.

Could Joseph have lost his memory? And be wandering somewhere without knowing who he was? Had he lost his mind? If he didn't return soon, she thought, they would need to enquire at the hospital, and the workhouse, the Asylum in Cheadle even. She shivered. And enlist the help of the police? Could Joseph have been arrested, even? But for what? And if not, would the police take any notice of the disappearance of a man of sixty, last seen in full possession of his faculties? They might spot him as they plied their beat, if a full description was put out. If he was still in Manchester, that was. Could he have gone abroad? Emigrated? What a daft thought. Why, and without a word?

At No.26 Diana had fed Will, had put him to bed and was singing him a lullaby. The two women watched as his eyes closed, jerked themselves open, slowly closed again.

And stayed shut.

They whispered, so as not to disturb him. Having only the one room was, not for the first time, a disadvantage.

Eliza found herself all the next day distracted. Accidents happened when you didn't keep your mind on the job, she knew; but somehow her thoughts kept slipping away to Joseph and what manner of thing could possibly have happened to him. And then they trailed off to Sarah and how she could survive without him. The loss of a breadwinner was not only a sorrow, it often spelt disaster to a family. Women were known to do impulsive things under that pressure, like marrying widowers with numerous children of their own, men whose only appeal was their wages.

At best Sarah would have to leave the house when the lease ran out; and rent a room as they did, and find work at the mill, one of the mills. It would be a sad ending to what had seemed a good marriage, a comfortable way of existence; but surely that couldn't happen?

The end of the day came. Diana returned to Waugh Street to take care of Will while Eliza hurried to Palmerston, counting the blessings of having a sister, two sisters, who could and would help when she was in need.

She knocked. The door opened to a Sarah with hope flooding her face, hope that turned to disappointment when she saw who was there.

'He's not come home then?' Eliza asked.

Sarah shook her head. 'And I've thought till I can't think no more. Come inside.'

'You look done up,' Eliza said with sympathy. They went into the living-room, untidy today, drab, ashes still littering the hearth, unlike its usual sparkling self.

"Aven't 'ad the 'eart in me,' said Sarah, sensing Eliza's register of the room.

'You sit down. I'll make us some tea. Now, tell me, any more thoughts as to what's become of him?'

'I've been over and over things,' said Sarah. 'And for the life of me I can't think.'

'Right,' said Eliza. 'Here's what we'll do.' And she began to put forward a plan of action. Tomorrow was Friday. When the boys had gone off to school, Sarah must go to the hospital and then to the police. They might have ideas of their own which could help. Sarah was alarmed at going to the hospital, but by this time the possibility of an accident had occurred to her too.

'Think. Is there anyone, any friend, family, he might be with?'

'There's the men at the brickyard,' said Sarah. 'But they didn't know anything on Saturday.'

'Better go and see them again, then. Do that first, afore you go to the police. If you tell them you're going to the police next, one of them might let slip something, not wanting trouble. And is there any of Joseph's family you can write to?'

'There's some in Spondon and roundabouts. That's where I come from, Spondon. And I'm thinking that's where I s'll have to go back to, if Joseph doesna turn up. I've plenty of family there meself. I s'll write to 'em and get 'em to ask his brother if 'e knows owt – e's a pub landlord there. No good really, writing to Mam and Dad: they can't read. But most of me brothers an' sisters can, so I'll get a letter penned. I'll do that tonight. Keep me mind from worriting.'

On the Saturday afternoon after work had finished, Eliza went to see her sister. Sarah-Ann was looking disgruntled.

'He's changed his job again,' she said. 'Was a bricklayer when I met him, then he was a dyer. Now he's going for a warehouseman. Why he can't settle to one thing I'll never know. And we're going to have to move. Over Ardwick way.'

That came as a blow to Eliza. 'So, you won't be able to look after Will for me, then?' She stared at her sister in shock.

Sarah-Ann looked both guilty and affronted. 'I won't that,' she said. 'But it's no good blaming me. He ain't going to do what I want. Don't rightly know what's come over him lately. This last week or two, and more since Joseph went, he's been right twitchy. Any more news of Joseph, is there?'

'There is not,' said Eliza, her mind buzzing. What was she going to do with Will when she was at work?

'And there's another thing,' said Sarah-Ann. 'Read it in the paper. Mills are going on short time.'

'I know,' said her sister shortly. 'Cheer me up, do.'

'Don't be sarcastic. I'm only telling you what's in the paper.'

'They talk about it all the time at the mill. Prices falling, stuff they can't sell increasing. Masters not making money. So what does the masters think to do but lay the workers off? And that's us. How are we supposed to eat if we can't get work?'

Sarah-Ann shrugged. 'Don't suppose they think of that. It's themselves they're bothered about. Got to have their carriages and their horses and their footmen. Just think of the shame, to say nothing of the inconvenience, of having only one footman.'

Eliza gave her a wry smile. 'I'd settle for that. Just the one,' she said.

February merged into March and still Joseph had not returned.

Operatives, across the cotton districts of Lancashire, pressed for wages to be paid – and thereby increased - by the length of the yarn they spun, instead of the weight. Their bosses threatened to close down the mills.

But it didn't happen, not that time. Those that did close found themselves out of pocket while others profited at their expense. 'And serve 'em right,' the workers grunted.

Sarah said she had decided. 'Joseph's not coming back,' she said flatly. 'I s'll leave a note with 'is workmates, but I'm going back to Spondon.'

'I shall miss you. Oh, I shall miss you so much,' said Eliza, putting her arms round her friend. 'You've been so good to me and Diana and Will.'

There was a pause.

'Why don't you come wi' me then?' asked Sarah. 'I've been thinking on and we could 'elp each other, look to't children between us. We could rent a cottage with the two of us, three of us if Diana came too, and 'elp each other out.'

Through Eliza's mind raced the pluses and minuses of this proposal. To stay here meant dealing with her current alarm at the prospect of Sarah-Ann moving to Ardwick and no longer being able to help her. Then there was the ever-present fear of short time and its concomitant drop in wages. Added to that was the gnawing worry of Diana's exposure to the predatory clutches of the overlooker. She knew also that if Sarah left without her, she would be losing one of the few people in Manchester that she had a fondness for.

To leave for somewhere new, yes, there was uncertainty in that, but she contemplated with excitement the prospect of having the run of a whole cottage. Three friends and their children making a life together. She warmed to the idea.

'It sounds good,' she said. 'But do you really want to live with us? What about your family? Wouldn't they want you living with them? And will they want me and Will? What'll they think of us?'

Sarah smiled. 'There's so many of 'em they'll hardly notice a few more. And there's so many of 'em they're used to what life throws at a body and they're none too stuck-up about it neither. You'll see. And Joseph's brother's there. Happen 'e can tell me something. An' I need to talk to 'im. 'E keeps the *Prince of Wales,* Thomas does. A bit above my lot are the 'Oskinsons.'

'What would I do for work? And Diana?' Eliza queried.

'Well, you wouldna believe it, but tiny little Spondon 'as a cotton mill of its very, very own,' said Sarah.

7
1882
INTO THE UNKNOWN

They left Manchester at the end of that March. Sarah, with no wage coming in, and having exhausted any small funds she had, could leave the move no longer. She had sold most of her furniture, already spent some of the proceeds, and needed what was left for the journey.

Sarah-Ann, now ensconced in tiny No.10 Slack Street in Ardwick, although she had benefitted from the move in the acquisition of some of Sarah's surplus pieces, saw them go with regret.

'Now don't fret,' Eliza had said, in an attempt both to reassure, and make her sister more satisfied with her fate. 'You've got your daughter and your husband and you've got his family in Ardwick; and there's the new baby to look forward to. You're quite well set-up really. We s'll write to each other, promise me that.'

And Sarah-Ann promised, though with less sincerity

than she might have shown, Eliza thought. She was getting big now, Sarah-Ann, her clothes straining. And however she wore her shawl, it did not disguise her shape.

'Three months to go,' she said. 'And I'm not looking forward to it, not the birth nor the lookings-after when it's over. It's hard being a woman.'

Eliza had kept the banknote her father had sent at Christmas. They had heard nothing further, though she had sent him a short note of thanks, purporting to come from her son and signed 'Your affectionate grandson Will.' The pound would ensure their fare to Spondon.

Sarah had written to her family of their coming and had received a cheerful, if wildly mis-spelt, response.

Diana was excited at the change in prospects: a whole house to themselves. Pleasant as the Booths had been, they were not family. Neither was Sarah, she reminded herself, but she was as near family as non-family could get.

'Besides,' she said to her sister, 'We s'll be all women. We can decide things for ourselves, without any man's say-so.'

'Except Will, and Sarah's boys,' Eliza pointed out.

Diana pulled a face. 'But they don't count, do they? Too young, they are.'

The girls at the mill wished them luck as they left at the end of that Saturday morning, pay in their pockets.

When they got to Waugh Street, they found Sarah and her boys Joe and Jesse already there, loaded with baskets and bundles. They went inside, picked up their own belongings; and the whole cavalcade moved off, with Mrs

Booth and her children waving from the doorstep. Eliza had a sudden feeling of lightness and freedom: another life awaited, and at the end of a journey which would be an excitement in itself.

The boys had been on a train before, said their mother, doing the reverse journey, from Derby where they'd been born, to Manchester. But that was when they were infants, too young to remember.

The boys were fascinated. They pulled their mother along the platform, hither and thither, jumping with excitement as they pointed out to each other wheels and funnels, shining brass and drivers with the aura of emperors; covering their ears ostentatiously against sudden bursts of hissing steam or the shriek of a guard's whistle.

Once in the train, checked anxiously by the adults for its destination so many times, they leaned their heads out of the window, standing on tiptoe to see even further, their words falling over each other in excitement. The slamming of heavy doors the length of the train, the whistle, the wave of the green flag, a jerk, the noise of metal against metal, the slow picking-up of speed, put them into an ecstasy. Sarah pulled down and firmly notched into place the heavy leather strap that hoisted up the window and pushed them into their seats, where they flattened their noses against the glass and stared.

The maze of brick petered out, the hovering cloak of smoke drew in upon itself until it was only a dirty blob in the distance, giving way to a strangeness of green. The boys wondered at animals never seen before which nibbled at it, at houses standing alone and lonely in the green wilderness, at the miles of empty green which opened up to them.

There were stations with strange names like Dove Holes and Whatstandwell, where people got off and others got on. There were two long viaducts where they flew like birds high above the trees. There were tunnels to count; and they quarrelled as to the number: thirteen, or was it fourteen, or only twelve?

Eliza thought of her father. She still suffered a vitriolic mix of hurt and despair when he, black with rage, came to mind, but she also remembered the fondness and admiration she had felt for him through her childhood. So she began, and Diana joined her, in telling the boys about that father, John Kirby, who had worked to build railways like this when he was a young man, before he had married their mother. He had built tunnels and stations and bridges too. And they told them the story that had made him a hero in their eyes, of how their father had saved England almost single-handed, by building a railway far over the sea in a country called the Crimea, when England was at war with the terrible Russian Bear.

That journey should never have ended, but it did and they were in Derby. Porters in uniform loaded up trolleys with the smart luggage of other folk, but left the little company to themselves to struggle up steps and over a new-built footbridge, then down stairs to another platform to wait for the Nottingham train.

'We shan't be long on this un,' said Sarah. 'What you've to do, boys, is watch out for the sign sayin' Spondon. Mind as you watch careful for that big letter S and tell us quick as you can, or we'll not get off and we'll be whisked away to t'other end o't line and that'd never do.'

The train came in and they climbed aboard. Having

settled themselves and set off, it seemed that the engine had hardly established its rhythm before it was slowing down and the boys shouting, 'There it is. Spondon. Spondon. We're 'ere, we're 'ere.'

They left the train, the boys with reluctance, glancing back at the monster as, in obedience to a whistle, it picked up speed and disappeared into the smoky distance.

'Not very far,' said Sarah. They trudged up Station Street and then Lodge Lane, towards a fine-looking church.

'St Mary's. Burnt down five 'undred years since,' Sarah informed them, 'along wi' most o't rest o't village. 'Bout the most exciting thing as 'as ever 'appened in Spondon. We carry on up 'ere.' She pointed.

Lodge Lane had turned into Church Hill. 'And 'ere we are,' Sarah said, turning to one of the houses that opened to the road.

'Sarah?' she called, lifting the latch and walking in. A plump woman came from the back, wiping her hands on an apron. She caught their Sarah in her arms, asking for any news of Joseph and uttering condolences. She then hugged her nephews-in-law before holding each at arms' length to encapsulate the whole boy, exclaiming the while what fine boys they were, indeed.

Eliza and Diana looked on, slightly uncomfortably, before Mrs Cope remembered her manners and greeted them too, as her sister-in-law introduced them. Then, to Eliza's gratification, she admired Will with the manner of one who thoroughly loved and appreciated the finer points of babies, no matter what their antecedents.

Tea was produced, the guests sat down as best they

could: it was not the biggest of houses. The boys had gone quiet, were drinking everything in with eyes growing ever larger.

'Now,' said Mrs Cope, 'you'll be wondering ... Your dad's put word out, and Mr 'Oskinson's done't same and there's a cottage in Butts Yard as is empty an' you can 'ave it. Not big mind, but cheap, which'll do very well at start till we sees 'ow things go. When as you've put your feet up for a minute or two an' you've drunk your teas, Sarah 'ere'll take you all round. I've got key. We've put a few things in there as'll do for starters, pallets like, an' a blanket or two. An' as it's Saturday there's a loaf an' a few bits an' bobs an' a pinch o' tea. Monday you'll need to turn up at Towle's an' get taken on. Won't be no problem there, them girls say.'

Out of the house then, restored, walking on up what had changed from Church Hill to Church Street.

'That's me dad's 'ouse,' said Sarah, pointing to No.8. 'Won't be no-one 'ome, now me mam's gone.'

Her companions already knew that Sarah's mother had died the preceding August.

'You'd never've known me am was an Irishwoman,' said Sarah after a minute or two of walking. 'Spoke as if she'd never left Spondon. Lived in Canada too, for years. She weren't me real mam though, you know. Me own mam died when I were still workin' at the farm here. Dad married again. Both on 'em were called Mary. John and Mary: nice, eh? Saved 'im getting' mixed up, half asleep, an' causin' offence, any road. I've got three proper brothers, besides another proper brother an' sister who died. And then, this second Mary as me dad married was a widow an' she brought Elizabeth, Rose an' Susan with 'er before 'avin' me three 'alf-brothers. Made quite a family; twelve on us, all told. One reason why I kept livin' out. Weren't a lot o' space at 'ome.'

'There's only the three of us,' said Eliza. ' There were more, but they all died, some of them before they'd rightly got here. Dad always wanted a son, but it were no good, they just died.

'My mam's sister, Sarah, now' she went on, 'she's got lots of boys. Mam used to tell him, "You should have married my sister instead of me." But I think he was fond of my mam for all that. That's where my sister got half her name from, from my mam's sister. For luck, maybe. Our Sarah-Ann hasn't had any boys yet, though. Perhaps this next babby'll be a boy.'

At the top of the incline, they were guided to turn right into Chapel Street. On the downward slope now, past a motley row of small cottages on their left, past an approaching shaggy-footed horse pulling a cart - 'Keep on't causey, boys' - until they reached almost the bottom, where, on their left, Butts Yard proclaimed itself.

Eliza had been looking at and assessing her new place of abode ever since they had left the station. There were trees here, rarely seen in Manchester or Birmingham, except in places reserved especially for them. There were shrubs and flowering plants too, where the fronts of some houses were set back from the roadway. Coal smoke rose lazily into the air from house chimneys, but it had not besmirched and blackened everything. The greenery put a sleepy, calming gloss over all: it softened hard edges.

Here were no regimented, identical streets criss-crossing at right angles, but a scattering of irregular pieces. Many of the houses were old; the larger houses often the shape of an oblong lying down, with a central door flanked each side by two, sometimes more, vertical oblongs for windows: some were three-storeyed. Others of the houses were of more recent build.

The houses were of different quality. Here, a big building surely housed the well-off; and needed servants for the household to run smoothly. A row of tiny cottages nearby spoke of labourers. A more spacious and more modern pair of villas hinted at folk bettering themselves. Came more clumps of cottages, some stretching up tall, some crouching; then a hint of a dwelling hidden behind high walls or dense greenery. It was as if the inhabitants of Spondon had, over many years, jumbled up the classes, as if Spondon had spent a long time quietly, and very slowly, adding to itself in an unconcerned, haphazard way.

Butts Yard was cramped and rather dark, some of its cottages minute, others somewhat larger.

'This 'ere is it,' said Sarah, taking out the key. The door creaked open and there was the tiny parlour, floored unevenly in tiles of red and black. A slightly larger kitchen cum sitting-room cum scullery, with a beaten earth floor, lay behind, from which stairs rose to the two bedrooms above. Someone, they noticed gratefully, had recently done a job with a broom.

'You and the boys have the front bedroom,' said Eliza. 'Me and Diana and Will, we'll go in the back.'

Someone had left a pile of old pallets in the parlour and these the boys helped drag upstairs. They looked above them into the tall space where the ceiling angled up to the thatch. It would be cold in the winter months.

Bundles were unwrapped and more bedding made an appearance. Clothes were piled in the corner. 'We'll need a rope,' said Diana. And one was found, having just been untied from a bundle. Some former occupant must have had the same idea, for two convenient hooks across the corner made by two walls provided places to which to secure the ends.

'Time for some food, I think,' said Eliza. 'Will must be famished. He's being very good.'

In the back room they found an old-fashioned and rusty range of diminutive size, but with an oven at the right and a tap denoting a supply of hot water on the left.

'Bit o' black-leading wanted there,' said Sarah, gazing at it critically. 'That wouldn't've passed in Mr Arkwright's 'ouse. Nor Mr Potter's at the 'All Farm neither, come to that. That's where as I started work, in Moor Street at the Potters', in't kitchen. Going on twelve I was then.

'But they was that particular at Mr Arkwright's, you wouldn't believe. Upper kitchen-maid I was there. Worked for 'em first 'ere in Spondon at the 'All - we passed by the 'All on our way up from't station - worked there after I left Mr Potter; and then stayed wi' them when they moved to Cromford. Big in Cromford, the Arkwrights. Big in England, come to that. Old Sir Richard was called the Cotton King. Built the grandest house in Cromford, Willersley Castle it were called, near 'is cotton mills. We lived in Rock 'Ouse, where Sir Richard lived before he decided to build his grand new Castle. Died before 'e could move in, though. Sad, really. Died at Rock 'Ouse. Anyway, Rock 'Ouse was grand enough for me. We had a footman an' a butler an' a coachman an' a lady's maid. I even 'ad a girl under me in't kitchen. And a cook over me o' course. She'd've made that under kitchen-maid polish that range o'er there till it shone. Now it's me own 'ouse, suppose I s'll 'ave to do it mesen.' She sighed.

'Well, let's hope it draws,' said Eliza. She found a back door and a lean-to, in which a very small pile of coals sloped against one wall. 'Best leave lighting the stove till tomorrow,' she said, coming back in.

Meanwhile Diana had come upon the promised loaf and a pot of jam and was looking for a knife. They ended up tearing pieces off the loaf; and delicious pieces they were, especially when dunked in jam. Will ate gallantly with the rest, though perhaps his face received as much jam as did his mouth.

'There's a pump over't sink,' said Sarah. 'One thing Spondon does 'ave is good, fresh water. Lots o' springs. I'll go across to me brother Charlie. See if 'Annah's got a cup or a jar she can spare. 'Annah's 'is wife, by the way. We'll 'ave to mek do till't boxes come or we can buy summat. An' tomorrow's Sunday, so that's no good.' She went out.

Eliza and Diana unpacked more bundles and baskets, retrieving a pan and a kettle together with some utensils.

Sarah returned with several glass jars of assorted sizes and instructed the boys to fill the kettle from the pump. 'Can't mek tea tonight, but we'll mek do wi' water.'

'Bless that 'Annah,' she went on. 'She gave me some rashers of bacon too. We'll 'ave 'em tomorrow, when as we've got a fire.'

A Victorian Miss

It was already dark. Sarah stood over her sons while they washed, heard their prayers and tucked them up on their pallets. They seemed too excited to sleep. Eliza did the same for Will. He too would have to sleep on the floor: at least he couldn't fall out of bed, though she worried that he might toddle across the floor and fall down the stairs. She part-blocked the doorway with a derelict wooden stool on its side.

Downstairs, light from a fire was gloomily absent. 'I'll step over to't *Prince o' Wales*,' said Sarah. 'Need to ask whether there's any news o' Joseph anyway.'

They had walked past the side of the public house as they turned into Butts Yard, its door recessed across a corner, its sign of the Prince of Wales' feathers proclaiming its existence to the passers-by of Chapel Street.

Mine host was currently Thomas Hoskinson, a younger brother of Joseph. Both had been born into the brick and tile-making trade. Both had moved peripatetically about the country from the tiny Warwickshire village of their birth, before finding work at Spondon's brick yard. Joseph, now a widower, had met and married Sarah Cope, her father a fellow brickyard worker at the time, and moved his new wife first to Derby, then to Manchester. His brother Thomas had stayed in situ and given up brick-making to become landlord of a hostelry.

Sarah was gone some while. Eliza and Diana sat on the earthen floor in the dark, shawls drawn close. The noises upstairs tailed away. It was very quiet.

'I'd like it if I wasn't made a piecer this time,' Diana said. She was, as usual, nursing her hand. Though she greased it often, the skin never seemed to heal.

`There was a click of a latch, a creak of a door; and blessed light. In came Sarah, bearing a hissing paraffin lamp.

'Sorry as I've been so long,' she said. 'Thomas's given us this. Says we can borrow it for a day or two till us gets to buy coal or candles. Or one of our own, though that'll be the day.'

The light, the extravagant light, made the darkness dance, driving it into corners, made a pool of comfort. They stretched their hands towards the welcome heat.

'Has he heard from Joseph?' Diana ventured.

'Nary a thing,' said Sarah shortly. 'Well, 'e knows where to find us. I left word. What could I do more? And Thomas sent this.' She set a pitcher on the floor.

'I'll get the jars,' said Diana, scrambling to her feet. It was beer; and good it was too.

Eliza was woken the following morning by Will pulling at her arm before falling wetly onto her. 'Will hungly,' he said.

For a moment she wondered where she was. Was she late for the mill? Then the previous day flooded back and she realised thankfully that it was Sunday. The whole day lay before them.

She relaxed, with a comfort-giving sense of having come to rest in calmer waters; and gave a luxurious stretch before reluctantly getting to her feet. Will's night-time nappy was hanging sodden between his knees. She removed it and sought round in the piles of clothing on the floor for another.

Perhaps here it would be easier to do some washing,

she thought. There was the pump over the stone sink in the kitchen and the boiler attached to the range for hot water, so long as they could afford fuel. Here, washing hung outdoors to dry might, just might, stay clean of smuts.

Dressed, and leaving Diana dressing herself, she made her way down to the kitchen, Will insisting on negotiating the stairs unaided, though she watched him, alert to rescue him if he fell.

Sarah appeared. 'They're still asleep, the boys. Let 'em lie a bit,' she said. 'So, what can us do about breakfast?'

'Best get the stove going first,' said Eliza. 'I'll go and get in some of that coal. And we'll need some kindling.' She looked round, saw nothing and disappeared to the lean-to. A few sticks of kindling hid in the gloom of a corner.

She looked around the dim space and up. A longer stick lay, almost hidden, across two beams and she pulled it out. A crown of moth-eaten turkey tail-feathers was bound round one end. She ran her hand down it, sloughing off detritus; and took it in with the kindling, calling out her find. Once inside, she tickled Will's ear to make him laugh; and then set to work on the cobwebs which fronded and dangled blackly out of reach of human hand, before handing over the task to Diana. 'Here, see what you can do.'

'Eh, leave them cobwebs!' It was Sarah. 'Cobs, they gets rid of bedbugs, lice and flies and such.'

'Well, we'll have nice, clean, new ones,' said Diana, continuing to twirl bunches of dust-ridden web around her feathers.

'We'll get the boys on gatherin' later,' said Sarah, as

Eliza began to build the fire ready to light. "Ere, I brought matches. I'll put the box on the mantel where Will can't get at 'em. Poisonous, they are and 'e'll put anything in 'is mouth these days, I've noticed.'

The match caught paper and then the dry kindling. Eliza fed the tiny flames until the heat told her it was time to use morsels of the coal. There was soon satisfying warmth. The kettle was refilled from the pump and placed on the iron-barred top, over the hottest part of the blaze.

'We'll use it for't tea,' said Sarah, looking for the 'pinch o' tea' that her sister-in-law had promised.

'There's these shelves,' she went on, running the tip of a finger over the wooden boards fixed to the wall, before looking critically at its blackness. 'They'll need scrubbing. We best make a list o' things we'm going to need. Soap's one. Scrubbing brush - though those'll come on Monday or Tuesday in't boxes, so we'll leave shelves till then.'

Sarah of course had had a house back in Manchester; and her household goods, even the remnants, had been too many to transport personally. The larger items she had sold. The piano, with much regret, had gone first: but she had had to sell anything not essential to keep herself and her sons fed with no income coming in.

The last of her household goods, essential, smaller, or unsellable things, had been sent on by rail. Eliza had added a few items of theirs that they couldn't carry. The boxes would arrive at 8 Church Street; but hopefully the carrier could be persuaded to bring them on to Butts Yard.

'An' the sooner the better,' she said.

The smell of frying bacon had brought the boys tumbling down the stairs. They sat on the floor with slices of bread upon their knees in lieu of plates, waiting. The bacon swam in fat and more bread was fried to a crisp. Eliza chewed up bacon for Will, who had some teeth but not enough. The bread she pulled into fragments and dipped them in tea and those he sucked and swallowed. Any bread remaining, the boys dipped into the jam.

'Now, we best get oursens ready,' said Sarah. 'We's going to Chapel.'

They had already learnt that, although in the anonymity of Manchester many people neglected Sunday observance, in Spondon folk went to either Chapel or to Church. 'Church we leaves to't gentry an' such,' said Sarah. 'Mostly, anyway. The likes of us are Chapel folk. It's friendly an' you'll meet everyone that way. An' we've got to find someone to mind Will.'

The Chapel was only a step up Chapel Street, it being responsible for the street's name. It was a Wesleyan Methodist Chapel, modestly ecclesiastical in red brick. They took their places, discreet smiles and waves being exchanged when people turned their heads; and the service began. There was a lot of singing, which particularly suited Diana. Will became bored and loudly cross and had to be taken out.

Afterwards they found themselves the centre of a crowd of chattering, hugging, inquisitive Copes and Cope appendages. 'Half the congregation,' muttered Diana.

Eliza was introduced as a widow, Mrs Kirby: Diana as her sister Diana Kirby. 'A cousin, the husband,' Sarah was heard whispering to a particularly inquisitive Cope with a long nose and sharp eyes.

Someone prodded forward a girl of eleven or twelve who had recently left school and was wanting occupation.

'This is our Martha.'

'See how she takes to Will,' said Eliza. 'Or more, how Will takes to her.'

The girl Martha picked Will up, took him to an open space and began to chase him gently, swooping him up when she caught him. Will soon got the idea and chuckled and ran till he fell down. Whereupon the little girl picked him up and soothed him into chuckling again.

'She's 'ad a lot o' practice,' her mother said. Martha was engaged to start on the morrow.

'Where's our school?' asked Jesse, the younger of Sarah's sons. Sarah had asked her father to register the boys at the National School – for to school they must now go, like it or not - and they were due to start the following day.

A few steps further up the street and they were there, another red-brick building. 'We can lie in bed till nearly school-time,' said Joe with glee. He was the elder of the two brothers.

'You'll be on time,' said their mother grimly. 'Mr Douglass'll see to that. Fair 'e is, but strict as well; and 'e keeps a lively cane. So watch it.'

'Where's this mill?' asked Diana.

'Well, it's not exactly in Spondon itself,' said Sarah. 'But it's only just over a mile away. An easy walk; and there's many folks as do it, some of me family as well. You'll find out tomorrow.'

Eliza looked around her and sighed. It might be the Lord's Day, but wet nappies beckoned. They had no soap as yet, so she took them out into the yard and rinsed them as well as she could under the big communal pump, after which she wrung them out and hung them on a clothes line which crossed the yard. Thank goodness they had all arrived with clothes clean from the preceding Sunday's public baths, she thought. And wondered too whether such facilities existed in Spondon.

'Not as yet,' said Sarah, when applied to. 'Got 'em in Derby. Don't open Sundays, though. Desecrating the Sabbath, they calls it.'

'They opened Sundays back in Ancoats,' objected Diana.

'Well, Derby's more godly,' said Sarah. 'And in Spondon, you'll 'ave to use a tin bath or a dolly tub. Unless you've an 'ouse with a proper bathroom in it. In which case you can 'ave as many ungodly baths on a Sunday as you likes.'

8
1882
BAND OF HOPE

The morning of Monday dawned dark and wet. They scrambled to rouse the fire which had been damped down the night before; and made a hasty pan of tea with the used leaves kept from yesterday. The water soon boiled, having stayed warm through the night. Bread was toasted, or rather hotted, in front of the flames. Will was to be allowed to sleep until Martha arrived, which, to Eliza's relief, she did just as they were leaving the house. She would make sure the boys were on time for school, she said. She seemed a useful little person, Eliza thought.

In the yard, doors were opening and shutting, clogs clattering. They joined the little group of workers which became larger as they entered Chapel Street and larger still the further they proceeded on their way. If she closed her eyes, Eliza thought, she could well be back in Ancoats.

'A mile, mile an' an 'alf mebbe, to't mill,' said Sarah, rallying her troops.

There was a short stretch of street, then a foot road, before they joined the highway.

'This be't turnpike, Derby to Nottingham,' Sarah told them.

As they went, she pointed out places of note. 'One o't Towles lives in that one,' she said, pointing to an imposing house. 'Solicitor, though. Nowt to do wi't mill.'

After a while, they turned to their right off the turnpike, then over a hump-backed bridge crossing a canal and a railway line.

'Derby to Nottin'am,' said Sarah, indicating the railway. 'One as we came on.' And, pointing back in the direction of the highway they had left, 'They do say that once - oh, an 'undred year ago, more, long before there were a railway, anyhow - some Frenchies was set to mend't road from Derby to Nottingham. They wasn't no ordinary Frenchies neither. They was gentry, wi' wigs an' ruffles. Prisoners o' war. Folks laughed at 'em, but they didn't do no stealin' or nothing. Funny, gentry havin' to mend roads.

'Oh, an' back there, on't turnpike towards Derby, was a murder once. Stone as marks it. Tell you sometime. But look, we're nearly there.'

They could see the mill, a four-square building of four storeys with small-paned windows and a tall, angular chimney. A lower extension stretched at right-angles to one side, its own chimney rising upwards. Oddly to Eliza's eyes, the mill was set in greenery. Water surged alongside. 'Mill race. From't River Derwent,' explained

Sarah.

'You do know everything,' said Diana, teasing.

'Well, I've lived 'ereabouts almost all me life,' said Sarah, bridling a little. 'And that's Borrowash.' She gestured to the cluster of houses.

'Smaller than Spondon,' said Diana wonderingly, a stranger to small places.

They were all taken on. Here it was men who worked in the Carding Room, each feeding nine machines at the same time. Eliza, citing her previous experience, was put onto the task that was the next step after carding, in what was termed the Drawing Room. As before, she was allotted a girl to follow until she had mastered the process.

The room was full of drawing frames, each holding a set of steam-driven rollers. The 'rovings', those narrow bands of fleece, which in Manchester had been the product of Eliza's work in the Carding Room, were fed over the rollers. From the first machine the rovings emerged as a rope, fluffed thick as a bell-pull but so soft, said Ann, her mentor, with pride, that it could be passed through the eye of a darning needle.

'Not as I've ever tried it mesen,' she admitted.

From there the rope entered a second machine, at greater speed and greater pressure; and from there to a third machine, similarly advanced. The fibres, as they progressed, were drawn out and compressed, lost their inequalities and became more uniform over the entire length.

Should a thread break, the machine immediately stopped, and the threads had to be once more joined. The speed of operation dazzled Eliza. It seemed daunting. She wondered what work her sister and Sarah had been given.

They met at dinner time. 'We'll get off to't shop,' said Sarah. 'Get us summat to eat now an' we can buy summat for supper as well.'

'Not much bread left,' said Diana. 'Have we got enough money for dripping?'

On the grocery shelves they spotted oatmeal. There was a sack of potatoes in a corner, onions in a box. Into the basket besides went dripping, tea, cheese, dried peas and a loaf to replace their stocks. The butcher's was not far off and there they found a tray of anonymous pies ready to eat and some cheap mutton bones of various sizes, meat clinging. 'Make a nice stew with those and onions and potatoes,' said Eliza.

Munching their pies, they sat on a convenient wall and counted their remaining money.

'We'll have to eat light to last the week,' said Eliza. 'And there's the rent to find when we get our wages.'

'We'll need coal,' said Diana. 'And paraffin.'

'Rush-lights', said her sister. 'Can't afford to keep using that lamp Mr Hoskinson lent us.'

'Milk'd be good,' said Sarah. 'For porridge tomorrow. We s'll 'ave to take a jug for that. There's a shop in Spondon keeps open all hours. Looks shut at the front sometimes but it ain't. We'll send one o' the lads round't back when we gets 'ome. Coal's what we really need.'

'It's fast running out,' said Eliza. 'What we've got, that pile of slack.'

Sarah was thinking. 'There's a coal-dealer,' she said. 'Up Moor End. Mr Watts, as me dad knows. Reckon 'e might let us 'ave some coal on tick, knowing me dad, like.

An' me, come to that. I'll go up there after work an' ask him. No 'arm in asking, is there? Can only say no, after all.'

The day passed comparatively quickly, being full of new, sometimes bewildering, experiences. They trudged home telling of their day.

Diana, much to her relief, had been told that they were up to strength on piecers. She had been placed in the room beyond her sister on a slubbing machine. Her machine, the one she was learning to use, she told them, carried twenty-eight bobbins. The now compact thread from Eliza's Drawing Room was twisted into even finer thread and wound onto a further bobbin. Two of these bobbins were then 'doubled', wound together onto a further bobbin for strength.

Sarah, who had no previous mill experience to offer, had nevertheless been put into the Reeling Room under the guidance of a relative of some sort named Fanny, who vouched for Sarah's application to duty.

'Yarn comes in and it's on bobbins,' Sarah told the others. 'But machine makes it into 'anks, skeins. It'll make forty 'anks in twenty minutes, that's how fast it goes. Right noisy an' all. When it's done an 'ank, it just stops, like magic. Fanny says an 'ank's four 'undred an' twenty yards. Then we 'ave to start it doing the next 'ank an' you can't waste even a second. You've to be there an' starting it up again. At end o't day, you've dealt wi' two 'undred an' ninety miles o' cotton, says Fanny. If you've worked at right speed. An' it's measured. There's a little thing on't side o't machine as tells 'ow many miles you've done.'

'Where does it go then?' Diana asked.

'Off to't dye-'ouse if as they want it black, say, says Fanny. Or to be bleached white if that's what's needed.'

At home they found the boys, eager to show their contribution to the household in the shape of a bundle of kindling. After school, Martha had shown them the way to the fields and explained what to look for; dry wood and fallen, not green on the tree.

'Martha says not to damage the trees or the 'edges 'cos you could get into big trouble.'

'An' it won't burn, neither, if it's got the sap in it,' put in his brother, showing off his new knowledge.

Will seemed contented. They let Martha go.

'Boxes 'aven't come,' said Sarah. 'Well, we'll just 'ave to manage. What about you two get us some tea an' I'll go an' see a man about some coal.'

She turned to the boys. 'Joe, you an' Jesse go down into Chapel Street an' cross over't road. You'll see a grocer's shop, Mr Fairbarnes. If 'e's not open, go round't back, knock at door an' say, "Sorry to trouble you. Please can me mam 'ave a pint o' best milk?" Be polite mind, or we'll not get no more. You can tell him your mam's John Cope's girl, 'ome from Manchester, if he asks. An' she sends 'er regards an' 'ow's Mrs Fairbarnes keepin' as she used to know. 'Ere's't money an' mind you look after it.'

The boys ran off, taking their biggest jar to hold the milk.

Sarah set off too, to knock up the coal dealer.

Eliza and Diana considered their purchases of the morning.

'Pea soup,' said Eliza. 'I put them in to soak the minute

we got home. Not long enough, but they'll have to do.'

'With bread to dip in it,' said Diana. 'And a smidgin of cheese. An' lots of pepper. I'll cut the bread into big fingers. What'll we use to put the soup in?'

'It'll have to be the jars again,' said Eliza. 'God bless Hannah. And at least we've got a pan. But we haven't got salt; and we haven't got your pepper, neither.'

The peas would have been better had they soaked all day as they should, but, after waiting for what seemed forever, the stage was reached when they became just about chewable. Diana had the idea of cutting a potato into tiny cubes and boiling them in with the peas a bit longer until they became a thickening mush. By then they were all so hungry, and Will yelling so loudly, that they would have enjoyed almost anything.

That was how Sarah found them as she came through the door, and gratefully accepted the proffered offering.

When the jars had been finger-licked clean and rinsed under the indoor pump, they sat for a while in front of the fire, risking opening it up for more warmth.

'An' 'ow was school, me ducks?' asked Sarah.

The boys shrugged. 'Same as usual,' Joe said after a while.

'Did thee do any writing?'

'A bit.'

'What about?'

'Dunno. Just writing.'

'A boy got all his sums wrong and the master put 'im in a corner with a big hat on and it 'ad 'dunce' written on it,' said Jesse all in a rush.

'Well, see it don't 'appen to you,' said their mother severely.

'Did you get any coal?' Eliza asked after a while.

"E'll deliver tomorrow. Slack an' some nuts. We'll pay 'im Saturday when we gets us wages.'

Jesse yawned widely and tried to stifle it. 'Time you lads were off to bed,' said their mother. And off they went with the most minimal of grumbles.

Eliza caught up Will, who was already slumbering, and took him upstairs.

'A blessed bit of peace,' she said when she came back down. The room was quiet except for the occasional tiny crackle or hiss from the fire; and dark except for its small glow of orange light to which all eyes were drawn.

'Who was Mr Butt?' asked Diana after a long silence.

'Dunno,' said Sarah. 'Oh, you mean 'cause it's Butts Yard? That weren't no Mr Butt. The Butts was what the place were called where they practised wi' bows an' arrows. Long, long ago. Mr Douglass told us all about it when we was at school – we did go to school when us parents could manage it. This must a' bin a field then and the men and the boys – sixty down to fourteen - they had to get themselves a bow, tall as they were, an' practise every Sunday after Church.'

Eliza tried to imagine a long-ago time with a field where now there were houses. 'When did it start, Spondon?'

'Well, dunno when it started, but it were 'ere when William the Conqueror wrote that big book, the Domesday Book. There was a church then like there is now, an' a priest an' a mill an' all of sixteen people.'

'It's not exactly grown a lot since then, has it,

Spondon?' said Diana. 'Not like Manchester. Mebbe Manchester was small once as well.'

They contemplated. Eliza tried to imagine a tiny Manchester set in greenery, just a few houses here and there. And the Cherwell running clear and sparkling instead of darkly putrid with dead and poisonous things. It seemed at odds with present reality. She began to feel quite fond of Spondon.

'But that first church burnt right down in 1340,' Sarah went on. 'In that fire I told you about. The Great Fire of Spondon, we calls it. We all 'ad to learn that date. That's 'ow as I know. They 'ad to build another one. The church you saw Saturday when we walked up from't station still 'as bits from that new-built one, the spire like an' the tower an' some o' the inside.'

Eliza got up. 'I s'll look over those mutton bits for tomorrow,' she said. 'An' leave them to seethe overnight with some onions. Might go off else. Pity we ate up all the soup, or that could've gone in as well. We'll have it tomorrow when we come off shift. If those boxes come, we can put in some salt. Food's not much without it. An' I'll make up some porridge with those oats and leave it just to stand warm over the fire for the morning.'

They left the food in the pans with a cover over, in case of mice. 'Or rats. Or cockroaches,' said Diana brightly.

The following day passed with each of the women feeling, as they acknowledged to each other, a little more confident in their mastery of their machines.

They walked home feeling cheerful, though the wind was getting up and the road was dark and wet. Life, they agreed, had taken a turn for the better.

'Like sailing into a calm harbour,' said Diana.

The household had three wage-earners. And, there being three of them, they could support each other. If one should fall ill - Heaven forbid - disaster would be held at a remove. They had a roof over their heads, a means of cooking and washing, a place to sleep. Hopefully today the boxes would have arrived and the few items within would add to their comfort. They could count themselves lucky. Added to that they had a little freedom, being at no man's mercy. Except that of their employer, Eliza thought.

'Why's it Towle's mill?' asked Diana, whose own thoughts must have followed similar lines. 'Is that who owns it? Some grand body?'

'Well, yes, it's Towle's mill. Mr John Towle. 'E's got other mills, over at Draycott. That's where 'e lives, Draycott, just up road. At the 'All. 'E's a widower, they say. Old now. But it's Mr Cade as runs our mill. 'E's the manager. You'll see 'im going about in a fancy gig. 'E lives in Spondon, at the 'Omestead. I'll show you sometime, when we go round that way. It's a grand old 'ouse, tall, wi' more rooms than there are 'ouses in Butts Yard.'

'Does he live there all on his own?' Diana was aghast.

'Eh, me duck, no. There's 'is father, 'e's the doctor. Very much respected is the doctor. An' there's 'is mam an' a proper posy o' sisters. An' a brother when 'e's not away at school an' such. An' a fair few servants, o' course. Needs a power o' dustin' an' scrubbin', a place that size. Anyway, 'e's alright, is Mr Charles. Same age as me, thirty-two. An' not married, neither. 'E'd be a right good catch, 'e would.'

'Chance'd be a fine thing,' sighed Diana.

Eliza felt a glint of amusement at this speaking beyond her years.

"Is mam were a Towle, from Draycott,' went on Sarah. 'S'pose that's 'ow 'e got to be manager. All in't family. Time was, the overlookers carried whips, but not no more. Couldn't abide slackin' in them olden days. Nowadays you'd likely get your wages docked an' some 'arsh words thrown at you, but there's not no whipping goes on. An't hours is shorter, so folk don't fall asleep like as they used to. Specially the little uns. Ducked 'em in barrels o' cold water, they did, if as they fell asleep. Some places, anyhow.' She fell silent.

Then, 'There's some o't old folk could tell you a thing or two. Right 'ard life it were in them old days.'

They had reached the little cottage in Butts Yard: home. And when they pushed open the door, there stood their boxes, still roped.

'I di'n't like to touch 'em,' said Martha. "Ope as I did right.'

'You did so,' said Sarah. 'You get off 'ome now. Where's the lads? Joe, Jesse? Come an' 'elp put things away.'

The boxes were untied and their contents revealed once more. A second shawl, looking somehow more shabby than its memory, another few blankets, an extra pan or two, a stock of assorted rags, some cups and plates, a bundle of rushlights and a holder, salt and pepper, a small shovel, scissors, a mousetrap, shoes that needed mending; all were disposed of in their appropriate place.

The savour of the pan over the fire drew them. The new arrivals, salt and pepper, were stirred in. Plates, proper plates, were handed round, spoons produced. They settled themselves, now comfortably raised above the beaten earth on Ancoats boxes. For a while conversation subsided.

'An' 'ow was school?' Sarah asked, when the plates had been rinsed and put back on the shelf; and Will had been taken sleepily to his bed; and they were once more sitting round the fire. It was a question they could count on her to ask.

'Alright,' said Joe.

'A boy got the cane,' volunteered Jesse. 'But I didn't,' he said, virtuously. 'I got all my sums right. 'Cept two. You don't get the cane like in Manchester. Not as much.'

'Well, that's a pity,' his mother said.

The wind had strengthened. They could hear its roar as it swept overhead. But they were sheltered in the yard, the houses standing like a squad of soldiers forming a protective square. Eliza gave a small shiver and bent to stir the fire a little.

'I know a story,' said Diana. The boys gazed at her.

'It happened many years ago,' she began, in a story sort of a voice. 'There was a young girl, a wealthy young girl, who lived in a splendid house. And she had seven brothers. They hadn't lived for long in the splendid house, because they were new to the neighbourhood. Well, about a mile away, there was another grand house; and the brothers got friendly with the owner, who was a young man like they were. And they all went hunting together and went to the races and gambled and diced and things like that.

'The brothers thought it'd be a fine thing to marry their sister off to this young man whose name was Mr Fox and who was said to be very rich and lived in the grand house, all empty except for himself. And they told him he could come a-calling. So Mr Fox did. But the sister didn't like him. She told her brothers, who were very cross and said she must do what they said. But the sister still didn't like him.

'One day, and the brothers'd been specially mean to her, she thought she'd soften them up by paying Mr Fox a visit. When she got to the great gloomy house, she knocked the door but no-one came. So she turned the iron handle. The door swung open with a groan and a creak and in she went. All the rooms were quiet and a lot of them were empty and dusty and the spider-webs were so thick over the windows that they shut out the light.

'Up the stairs she went and through the rooms she went. And up to the attics she went. And she came to a huge oaken door studded with great iron bolts which could be barred to keep anyone from getting out. So, she pulled the bolts. And the door opened.

'And inside were bones. Leg bones and arm bones and finger bones and head bones. And dresses, all torn and dusty, with nasty dark stains on 'em.

'And just then she heard the great front door opening. And a scream. And Mr Fox was hauling a lady up the stairs. So the sister hid, as small as she could be. And Mr Fox pushed the lady into the room with the bones and there was a most terrible screaming.

'And the sister sneaked out of the great house and fled home. When her brothers came, she told them the story, and showed them one of the head bones that she'd brought with her, with the long golden hair still on it and the black lips drawn back in a terrible grin.'

Diana stopped talking. Her audience was silent.

'And then,' she said, 'there was a knock at the door. It was the young man come a-calling. And the seven brothers picked up their seven swords. And they cut Mr Fox into a thousand pieces.'

Eliza smiled inwardly: she knew the story well, it having been one of her mother's and one which rarely failed to impress.

'An' now it's time for your beds,' said Sarah firmly. 'Say goodnight an' thank you for the story. Get washed an' say your prayers and into bed.'

The boys went out into the windy blackness of the yard to find the dunny, keeping, Eliza thought, rather close together.

9
1882
SETTLING IN

Saturday morning was over at last. A whole day and a half without toiling for others lay before them.

Once home they laid out their wages, having already decided to pool their money for the benefit of all. First there were repayments: to Sarah's father for paying for the boys' first week at school, to Thomas Hoskinson for finding the first week's rent, a whole florin to Mr Watts for the coal he'd given them on tick. Almost everyone in their walk of life lived hand to mouth: to lend was to deny oneself and a loan must therefore be repaid promptly. Or, when you were in need next time, help would not be offered.

Little piles were made: so much for food, so much for rent, for the boys' schooling, for Martha's wages, for necessities such as coal, matches, soap, a broom. Anything left over, or left over by the end of the week, would accumulate for replacements of footwear or clothing, or furniture, if and when such could be afforded. Hopefully they could also build up a cushion for emergencies, those events which came when least expected and which could devastate an improvident household; even, indeed, a provident one, but one must not think too closely of that.

A shopping list was decided upon. Diana would go with the boys to execute it and make their presence further known in the village.

Both Sarah and Eliza had washing to do and did it together, using hot water from the range, carried in a pan to the shallow stone sink under the small-paned window that looked out over the yard.

'There's young nephew Charlie playing about with his friends, an' little Ada with 'im. Let's take Will out there. Save 'im getting in our way. Ada's 'is age an' Charlie can take care of 'em. We can see 'em from here, anyway.'

So Will was deposited in the yard, with strict instructions to six-year-old Charlie not to let him out of the yard into the dangers of Chapel Street.

'It's the horses. He does love them so, but they're not always looking to their feet,' explained Eliza. 'An' then there's cart wheels o' course. Don't want my Will run over by a great big wheel. Nor your Ada, come to that.'

Charlie and an older girl promised to take care of the little ones. And the little ones could be heard giving squeals of delight as a game involving running and hiding and catching was most lengthily played.

Washing washed and rinsed and wrung and hung up to dry, Sarah said it was time she visited her dad.

'I s'll come with you and bring Will,' said Eliza. 'I'd like to thank your dad for his help, for being so good to us all.'

So off they set, with a Will initially reluctant to be dragged from the excitement of his game, but who soon found solace in all the things to be seen on the short trek between Butts Yard and Church Street.

'We'll go down the 'All Dyke for a change,' said Sarah. 'Same distance, more or less, shorter even.'

They went the few yards up Chapel Street till they had reached the Chapel; and opposite it turned left down an unpaved way between high walls. Will found a puddle to stamp in and Eliza dragged him away, tut-tutting at the splashes to his frock. He found another puddle.

'Spondon 'Ouse that side,' said Sarah, gesturing to her right. 'And the Old 'All that side,' waving to her left.

At the bottom of the dyke, they turned right and were soon in Church Street. They were welcomed in and Sarah gave her father the moneys owed, while Eliza expressed her thanks for all the help that had been given.

'Eh, me duck, never fret,' said Mr Cope, tamping the tobacco in his pipe. 'I've known troubles mesen. There's nowt new under't sun. An' 'ow're you gettin' on down't mill?' he asked, turning to Sarah. 'Our Fanny says as you're doing grand.'

'Could be worse,' said Sarah. 'Least it's regular hours, so you knows where you are. Not like bein' in a great 'ouse where the master might bring back a few friends when you's just off to bed an' you 'ave to start workin' all over again and be up next morning betimes. Mind you, in service you do get your food an' a uniform.'

Will on the homeward journey found a new puddle.

A Victorian Miss

'It'll dry,' said Sarah, looking at his frock. 'Most of it's on 'is pinny anyhow. Mebbe you can sponge the muck off.'

'So your dad's at the Brickworks. What do your brothers do?' Eliza asked.

'William, 'e's the next one down from me, lives on Church 'Ill. You met his wife, Sarah, last week, day we came to Spondon. 'E used to work on't railway but now he's at Colour Works.

'Then there's 'Erbert, shows no signs of ever getting married. He's out lodgin' in Stanley 'Ighway. 'E was at the Brickworks, with me dad an' me 'usband Joseph, but now he's at Colour Works wi' William.

'Charlie, you know 'im, 'im as lives in Butts Yard. 'E's married o' course an' 'e works at Colour Works as well. Big thing, the Colour Works, for't men. Down near't station, it is - them buildings wi' three big chimneys. Colour Works an't Railway, those are't main jobs for men. Not so much the Brickworks no more. An' the Cotton Mill, that's more women than men.

'The three littlest boys, they live wi' me dad. Two're still at school; an' John, the eldest, he's just left to go labouring.

'Then there's Rose, me stepsister. Born in Canada, she was. She's getting married Christmas Day so she won't be livin' wi' me dad much longer. Be livin' in Derby.

'Elizabeth, the eldest, she's been married a good while now. Lives in Newton in Lancashire. And there's Susan, the young un. She's an 'ousemaid at The Croft, boarding school in Church Street, just near me dad's. She lives wi' me dad when she's not 'ousemaiding. Shall I tell you about all me uncles? An' aunts o' course? An' cousins? An' nephews an' nieces?'

135

'Tell me another time,' said Eliza, who had become somewhat bemused. Sarah grinned.

The cotton thread, doubled, twisted, which they so arduously made, was later turned into cotton lace, they learned. Sometimes it became trimmings such as collars or cuffs or inserts, or it might make dressing-table sets, or table-cloths or even curtains. Most of their thread fed the Nottingham market.

Long gone were the days when people had made lace by hand in their own homes. Once, a girl might well start at five years old and become fully proficient with her pillow and prickings, pins and multiple bobbins, threads of cotton or silk, by the time she reached sixteen. Now the machines had taken over.

The days slipped past. The bluster of March transmuted into the raw sunlight and sharp showers of April, which softened into May. It was now a pleasure to walk to work through lanes singing with birds, frothing with hawthorn and cow parsley.

Came June; and to return in the evenings, in the stillness of the lingering heat, pulled at something in Eliza's heart. There was an absence, a deep longing. She acknowledged, though only to herself, that she wished she was a-courting again; and felt a deep sadness that, besmirched as she was, wicked as she was, this could never happen.

Nothing was heard of Joseph Hoskinson. It was as if he had been spirited away; and with each passing week it seemed less and less likely that he would ever return.

More of Sarah's family were encountered, at Chapel, at work, in the village shops and in the houses of other relatives. Eliza had now met two of Sarah's brothers and two of the Hardy girls, the daughters of Sarah's stepmother. 'An' very welcome they were,' said Sarah, 'after me being the only girl.'

Brother Herbert was elusive. "E's a bit on't shy side,' apologised Sarah, when they'd visited her dad one Sunday after Chapel; and a male sitting in the far corner had suddenly risen to his feet and was past them and out of the door.

"E likely thinks you're above 'im, being a foreigner like, from Manchester an' that,' said her father.

He had something for them, a couple of orange boxes and a tea-chest. 'Do for keeping things in, mebbe,' he said.

In Spondon, everyone spoke like Sarah, the girls had realised. The two of them stood out like sore thumbs.

'I suppose,' said Diana, 'that we've lived in so many places that we've got sort of worn down, our voices, I mean. All the corners've rubbed off an' we don't speak like anywhere in particular.'

In July, Sarah-Ann, to whose sisterly discretion Eliza had at last confided the secret of Will's paternity, wrote to say that Alfred George, her brother-in-law - and Will's father - had joined the police force. He was settling down, she said, becoming more staid and reliable. She did not mention her husband, only that she was dreading the birth of her coming child.

In August, Sarah-Ann wrote to say she had had the

baby. It was another girl, named Mary after her husband's mother. The letter was brief: she did not express any happiness; and Eliza felt, at the base of her mind, a gnawing foreboding that she did not give voice to.

At the end of that month, a basket appeared on their doorstep overnight. Diana found it and brought it in. It was a rough-woven affair of withies, containing a couple of dozen field mushrooms, white as white.

'Someone was up betimes,' said Sarah.

September saw Eliza turn twenty-six. It was a Saturday, a good day to enjoy an anniversary, though little celebration took place on birthdays: money was for necessities and could not be squandered.

Not only was the 16th a Saturday, it was also a day of mellow September sunlight, warm and dry. After shopping had been done the women decided to take Will for a walk. Joe and Jesse by this time were familiar with their environs, knew their way about the footpaths and fields. They would be the guides for them all to gather the week's kindling; and all would pick late blackberries. A pie could be made for Sunday. If they picked enough, the berries could be turned into jam to join what they already had. They had the jars and, if they stinted themselves to afford the sugar, the jam would store against the winter.

They set off up Chapel Street, turning right immediately past the Chapel up Chapel Lane, a track where the cottages soon petered out, giving way to hedgerows and fields.

Will, when shown what to do, began to find pieces of stick which he gave to whomever took his fancy at that particular moment, running importantly back and forth and covering a distance three times longer than he needed to.

When they at last found a patch of brambles, his pot never contained more than half a dozen sorry-looking fruit, whilst his fingers, lips and chin grew ever more stained.

'Well, he'll eat less tea,' said Diana.

They kept walking, by footpath and pieces of lane until they came to what Sarah told them was the Lees Brook. Will was keen to test this substance and Eliza had to hang onto him to stop him surging forward and plunging in. Will had an independent spirit, she was beginning to realise.

'Floods sometimes,' Sarah said of the brook. 'Starts in Locko Park an' runs east towards Chaddesdon an' Derby. Joins up wi' a couple of other brooks an' then goes into the River Derwent - "an' the Derwent runs into the Trent an' the Trent runs into the Mersey an' the Mersey runs into the sea",' she chanted in a sing-song voice. 'That's 'ow we learned it at school.'

'So that bit of water there,' said Diana, pointing at a white-frothed patch,' will end up in the sea?'

'That's right,' said Sarah. 'If it don't have an accident along the way, anyhow. Get drunk by a cow or something.'

They came across a patch of reeds.

'That's a bit o' luck,' said Sarah. 'We're just about to run out o't last lot. Lads, look to the tallest an' the fattest. Couple o' dozen 'd be good.'

The boys began picking with enthusiasm.

They spotted a crab-apple tree in a hedgerow. The fruit

was still unripe on the branches but they noted its position for another visit in a few weeks.

They were glad to reach home, feeling weary but exhilarated by the air and the sunshine and the freedom of it all. Will, tiring sooner than they, after wailing and trailing for a long time, had sat down and refused to move. Even when they walked off, leaving him to a lonely fate, he had stayed stubbornly where he was and finally had to be rescued and carried back.

As they went through the door, Eliza caught sight of something. She bent to pick it up. It was a tiny feather of an intense blue, crossed with black bars.

'It's a jay's wing-feather,' said Sarah. 'Pretty, aren't they?'

'Beautiful,' Eliza said, turning it round. 'I wonder how it came to be here, inside?'

'Well, we didn't lock the door,' said Diana. 'Anyone could have opened the door and laid it down. Or most likely it drifted in sometime when the door was open and we didn't notice before.'

'Mebbe I'll wear it on my Sunday hat,' Eliza said.

The reeds were put into a water-filled jar; and that evening they set to stripping the green outside skin from the pith. It was fiddly work.

'We've often bought these,' said Eliza, 'but we've never made them. Not many reeds in a town.'

'Need to leave one long strip of green on,' said Sarah. 'makes 'em stronger, like.'

'Shall I get the fat warm?' asked Diana.

'They'll need to dry first. We'll leave them in the

warm till tomorrow at least. Dip them tomorrow night, maybe.'

The house had become more comfortable over the months: the walls were lime-washed against vermin, a deal table, though heavily scarred by previous use, had been bought and scrubbed to whiteness; and they had three ill-assorted chairs to add to the boxes. Boxes unwanted as seats had become cupboards. A dresser, snatched from a fate as firewood, a brick substituted for one of its legs, held their crockery. The rich sometimes replaced their furnishings, or old people died and what their relations didn't want or need was sold for what it would fetch.

'I can teach you how to make rag rugs,' said Diana to Sarah. 'If you don't know already, that is. Our mam taught us. We need some coarse sacking for a backing and as many rags as we can get. Old stockings are good. I've got a pair of blue cotton ones and I've mended them so many times that I can't mend them anymore. We can tear them into strips and loop them through the sacking. You can make really pretty ones if you've an eye for colour, like our mam had.'

Sarah was enthusiastic. 'I 'ave made 'em, but not for a long time. A rug in front o't fire would be a comfort. An' one each for't bedrooms. We could do a bit of an evening. I'll ask around for rags.'

'Well, there's enough of you Copes. Should get quite a pile,' said Diana. 'If they're not making their own, that is.'

Coming out of Chapel the following day, Sarah

approached her sister-in-law, brother William's wife, the young woman who had welcomed them to Spondon the day they had arrived; and confusingly named Sarah.

The second Sarah had two small boys in tow and a slightly older girl. The children stood and stared while Sarah One made her request for rags. Sarah Two promised to see what she could find. 'Mind you,' she said, 'I use nearly everything meself in one way or t'other.'

'An' 'ow's little Adolphus?' asked Sarah One.

''Ow are you, Adolphus?' Sarah Two turned to one of the boys who didn't speak. 'We've 'ad 'im a few months now, as you knows, but 'e still don't say much. Daft name, Adolphus. Adolphus McDowell Ross, 'e is. A right mouthful. But that's what 'is mam called 'im so that's what us sticks to. Or rather, it's what 'is dad called 'im, cos that's 'is name too.'

She turned to Eliza and Diane, 'We looks after 'im cos 'is mam's dead, last June, in Derby. Only twenty, she were, poor lamb. An' is dad's a sailor an' can't look after 'im isself. An' anyway 'e's gettin' married again this month. Wrote an' told us, but didn't ask for't lad back. Mebbe't new one doesna want 'im. We gets a bit for 'is keep anyhow. Comes in 'andy enough.'

'E's a nice little thing, anyways,' said Sarah One, ruffling the boy's hair.

'Our William gets on well wi' 'im. Same age, they are. An 'e's no trouble like, specially now they're all at school,' said Sarah Two. 'Well, must get on. Come on, me ducks.' And she marched off with her brood.

'She's got a good 'eart,' said Sarah, looking after her sister-in-law. 'She's right fond o' that little lad, though you might not think it sometimes. Poor little thing.'

'I can see as I mightn't come as such a dreadful surprise,' said Eliza, her sense of being an unwanted outcast weakening a little. 'If they do guess I'm not a widow-woman.' She realised a feeling of kinship with a seemingly unwanted young Adolphus and felt a surge of kindness towards him.

'As me dad says,' said Sarah, 'There's nowt new under't sun.'

Eliza had contrived to add the jay's feather to her Sunday bonnet, though no-one had remarked on it. It was pretty though, she thought. Such a vivid blue.

Life continued on its course of calm. Sarah had told them that little of any moment, apart from the Great Fire, had ever befallen Spondon, which was somehow comforting.

'But you said there was a murder!' Diana suddenly remembered, one October evening and the nights drawing in. 'That first day we went to the Mill. You said you'd tell us sometime, but you never have.'

'So I did,' said Sarah, remembering. The boys crept close.

'Well, 'e lived in Church Street, where me dad is. I knew 'im, 'cause 'e stood out like, on account o' walking wi' a limp. Dot an' carry one, we used to say, us children. Cruel, we were, 'cause 'e were an 'armless feller. Blew organ in't Church. Cleaned it an' all. Framework knitter by trade. One June night, 'is daughters come back from't Mill, find 'im reading't Bible. 'Bout eight o' clock, that were.

"Well, better go off ter get our Joe's washing," 'e says.

- That's 'is son, see, as is servant to Mr Moore at Appleby 'All - an' off 'e sets. 'As a pint of ale an' a bit o' bread an' cheese at Plough, then goes on, down to't turnpike, turns right to Derby - where we'd turn left to't Mill an' Nottin'am. Must a got to wherever 'is son Joe'd left the 'amper wi't dirty washing, an' then 'e turns around an' starts back.

'Anyway, two chaps was goin't same way as 'im coming back, Derby to Nottingham, along turnpike, an' they sees a man lyin' in't roadway. Looked at 'im, thought 'e must be drunk. An' is face were all black, they said. Cause it's night-time, o' course, an' they can't 'ardly see. They picks up 'amper wi't clothes in, an' carts it a bit further up road. But them clothes stank, they said, so they drops it again.

'Then, gone midnight, along comes a man driving a carriage, going t'other way, to Derby station to collect 'is master, Mr Cox, an' take 'im 'ome to the 'All, 'ere in Spondon. An' another man with 'im, getting a lift, a keeper.

First they finds an 'at. Then some clothes an' an 'amper. They picks 'em up. Bit further along they sees a man lying. Stop. Look careful at 'im. This lot got a light, see. Skull bashed in, broke, ear to ear, blood all over.

'Go on to Derby, tell police; an' them not too bothered. Coachman picks up 'is Master, Mr Cox, to take back to Spondon, an' Mr Cox sends out a cart wi' two men to bring Enoch Stone – cos that's 'is name - back 'ome. Surgeon – an' that's Mr Cade, father of our Mr Cade at the Mill – gets 'im put to bed, tries 'im wi' brandy, but 'e can't swaller, sits with 'im all night. But 'e's a goner.'

'An' who did it?' Diana asked, eyes wide.

Sarah shook her head. 'That, they never did find out,' she said. 'Big reward, there was. Government give £100, £20 from people in Spondon. Could read about it in every newspaper in England, they said. An' 'e'd never an enemy in't world. 8d missing from 'is pocket, clothes what'd been in't 'amper. An' both 'is boots. Odd uns.' She gazed at them.

'They might murder us,' said Joseph, wide-eyed.

'Nah,' said Sarah. Then, as afterthought, 'Only if as you're very bad.'

'But you said as Enoch were a good man,' protested Jesse.

'Time for bed,' said his mother briskly; and shooed them off, like geese, making them giggle.

'Sometimes,' she said, a while later, 'I should learn to keep me mouth shut.'

In November, something else bad happened. True, it was not in Spondon, but near enough, some twenty miles north. In the village of Clay Cross, families depended on the mining of coal for their daily bread, son following father down the pit as soon as school had been left behind.

At a quarter past ten on the morning of the 7th of November 1882, there came an enormous blast of sound. In all the cottages, women stopped what they were doing and stood, alert with dread. Men who'd come off the night shift were roused from their beds. A dense cloud of smoke, bricks and wood had shot from No.7 shaft of what the locals called the Catty Pit, to rain down all around. Rescuers who ran to the pit-head had to wait, could do nothing, until the air cleared.

Sooner than was prudent, down they went, many

beaten back by the suffocating fumes of as yet unexploded firedamp, forced against their will to return: some would never properly recover.

All that day men laboured in deep workings to retrieve the dead, then through the night and on again. The last of the bodies was not brought up until the Friday, brought up on wooden planks, wrapped and laid onto a procession of carts, thickly bedded with straw, which rumbled up to the Queen's Head Hotel for the corpses to be identified by distraught relatives.

Forty-five men and boys lost their lives, some overcome by the gas, others burnt to blackness by the fire which followed its explosion. The oldest was fifty-three, the youngest fourteen. Two families each lost a father and two sons. Two brothers died along with their uncle. Thirty women were made widows, livelihoods destroyed.

Thousands attended the funerals. An inquest found no-one responsible. It recommended that safety-lamps, instead of candles, be used in future in the deep parts of the mine, that a safety inspection be carried out more than once on each shift; and that the present method of ventilation, a furnace, should be improved on. A fund was opened for the survivors. The Clay Cross Colliery Company contributed £500.

Mill-work, brick-making and dyeing seemed snug ways of earning a living in comparison.

December came and with it Jesse's birthday. He was six. For tea, they had crumpets, spread with butter, a real treat. Jesse had helped to make them on the griddle and was much praised.

Three days afterwards came Will's birthday, a

A Victorian Miss

Thursday. He was two. Sarah was up first that morning. When Eliza and Diana came down, Sarah had something in her hands. She showed it, a wooden cart with four wheels, to be pulled along by a string. It was a cart in which a boy could collect things and pull them along with him as he went about his day.

'What a lovely cart,' Diana said, reaching out for it and turning it round in her hands. 'Look, someone's made it so carefully. Who on earth could it be from, though?'

'Don't say,' said Sarah. 'Found it in't lean-to when I went out this morning for coal. Was at back in't dark. Only saw it by accident. Could've been there for a day or two. Do you think it's meant for our lads? Jesse and Will, anyway, because of birthdays an' them being younger? Or for just one of 'em?'

'Well, we'll not wake them up now,' said Eliza. 'We'll give it them when we get back tonight.'

On and off through the day the cart returned to her mind, but the identity of its maker became no clearer.

It had been dark and drear that morning as they walked to work that December morning, and the prospect on their return journey was no better. The weather had suddenly warmed, though whether desirable or not was to be debated. The crisp cold of the previous fortnight had made trees, grass and bushes sparkle; and on the previous Saturday they had been able, if not to skate, to slide on the flooded, frozen waters of the Lees Brook. Joe and Jesse and Will had slid and skidded and had been happy.

Eliza's thoughts went back to the winter before last, in dreary Ancoats, and Will some six weeks old. She remembered how Sarah had recounted her skating tales;

and how she, Eliza, had had visions of Will swooping on ice, and of how impossible it had seemed then.

How much had happened since the watershed of her sister's wedding, she thought. New lives had come into the world. Manchester had been replaced by Birmingham, then Manchester again, then Spondon. Friends had been made, friends had vanished. From a position of near-desperation she, at any rate, had reached independence and near-contentment, and she thought that Sarah and Diana felt much the same. Life had become incomparably better.

She was looking forward to presenting the boys with their cart. A spark of happiness rose inside her.

'Will. Look, Will. Just look at this.' Eliza produced the cart from behind her back and held it towards her son. Will came forward and reached out for a wheel, which he made spin. Eliza put it on the floor. 'Look, you can put this in it.' She produced a piece of stick. 'And then you can take the stick for a ride, like this.' She demonstrated. Will took the string and looked back at the cart as it rolled along behind him. He took it all around the room before picking up a piece of coal and adding that to the load; and then a stray dead leaf which had found its way inside and a thimble which had rolled under a chair.

Jesse watched him.

'You can play with it as well,' they told him. But he screwed up his face and took no part.

That night Will refused to be parted from his new toy, insisting it lay by his bed. Small items that went missing thereafter were looked for in Will's cart; and often were found amongst the load. Eliza was to tell everyone she met how much Will loved his new toy. But no-one knew its source; or if they did, they were not going to tell.

A Victorian Miss

10
1883
ANOTHER YEAR TURNS

The Mill closed as usual halfway through Saturday. It was, as far as weather went, a most unpromising day: morning rain had turned to sleet. All the same, the group from Butts Yard were determined to enjoy themselves. For a Christmas treat they were going to Derby; and going, moreover, by train. The older boys were ecstatic and Will had caught their mood.

Sadly, the distance from Spondon to Derby had grown no longer since their first trip; and no sooner, it seemed, had the heavy door been slammed to by the guard, than the three glorious miles were coming to a halt as they steamed into Derby station. Still, the station and its glass-covered, echoing heights, its vast locomotives obedient to the shriek of a guard's whistle, hissing and heavily huffing as they moved their bulk, the harsh clankings of straining metal as they glided ponderously in or out, were a source of limitless fascination for the boys. The conclave was filled with a further sound, the sound of soft cooing, a sound that emanated from dozens of wicker baskets piled up on platforms or on trolleys, as uniformed and waistcoated porters whisked them from one platform to another. The boys would have stayed all day, but were pulled away by a combination of carrot and stick by their elders.

Down endless, sleet-sodden Siddals Road, beginning between two lines of uniform railway cottages, they tramped, scorning the newly-instigated horse-drawn trams which out-sped them; to come at last into the thronging centre where whispers of an ancient identity were held in streetnames: Sadler Gate, Friar Gate, St Mary's Gate, Iron Gate.

The streets were choked with waggons, phaetons, gigs, cabs, omnibuses, chaises; vehicles of every description spurting icy wetness from their wheels, so that each pedestrian was anxious to pass on the wall side. The all-pervasive smell of horses, present though not overpowering in Spondon, was strong here. Passage from one side of a road to the other, through the mire of dung and straw and slush was feasible only at crossing-places, kept clear by scrawny urchins who would sweep diligently before you, try to catch your eye, and then raise their tattered caps in hope of reward.

The boys stared at rows of fully-feathered turkeys, ducks, geese, hanging upside-down outside the shop by their scaley legs, their necks dangling. They gazed in, at pork pies the circumference of the largest of dinner-plates and tall as a stove-pipe hat. They wandered among displays of children's books (half-price), of Japanese lanterns, fancy sweets and bright paper rolls called cosaques. These, Diana told them, were to be pulled between two people, whereupon there was a splendid explosion, the insides fell out and you both scrabbled for what you could grab: a motto, a toy, a sweet, a hat.

The women were entranced by the Modes de Paris at Miss Askey's in St Mary's Gate. Tight, boned bodices and long, fitted sleeves showed off tiny waists, their daintiness emphasised by a bustle behind. In Iron Gate they longed to own at least one item from the display of flowers, feathers, mantles, millinery, all the 'latest novelties and designs'. Those bonnets, oh such bonnets! In St Peter's Street they gazed with awe through the plate-glass windows of the new-built, and still novel, department store of Thurman & Malin; and at the carriage-folk passing in and out, so elegantly dressed.

The market heaved wetly with sightseers, the brass strains of Christmas carols rising above a turmoil of voices. The gas-lamps were being brought to life one by one by a man with a long pole, naphtha torches flared and hissed and spat at the falling sleet; and here they bought for their own Christmas dinner. They were standing in front of a stall, debating the merits of a rabbit versus a piece of ham, and wondering could they afford a chicken, when a voice from behind said, 'Eh me ducks, if it ain't Mrs 'Oskinson, and Mrs an' Miss Kirby. A rare treat to see you an' all. Ray o' sunshine on a reet daft day. An't lads too! Enjoyin' yersens, young gents?'

As the boys half-grinned and squirmed, Sarah

introduced the interloper. 'This is Mr Woolley. Alfred as was, when I were at school alongside 'is big brother 'Enry, as I'm sure 'e won't mind me telling yer.'

They all shook hands, Eliza and Diana a little shy.

'Fred lives in Spondon,' said Sarah. 'Sorry to 'ear as you got troubles, Fred. I 'ear as you're still on Stanley 'Ighway.'

'Wi' me mam. I am that. Still, 'er's gettin' on; an' it's good as 'er's got a body as'll look after 'er. An' I 'ope yer wunna mind me asking, but I 'eard as you'd troubles yersen, an' I 'opes as yer's gettin' through 'em.'

'Well, good on yer to ask, Fred. You've gone an' lost a wife an' me, I've gone an' lost an 'usband. Puts us on a level, like.'

'Anytime as you wants an 'and, just let us know,' said Fred after a while. 'Must be gettin' on now. Pleased to meet all on yer. And a very 'appy Christmas to the lot o' yer.'

All concurred and they shook hands. Fred left, with a lift of his cap.

'Good-looking chap,' said Diana. 'Well set-up. What happened to his wife?'

Sarah made a face and shook her head. 'Dunno exactly. She went back to live with 'er mam an' dad. Took the three little uns with 'er an all.'

'Must've been something important,' said Diana, 'for a woman to leave her husband. How's she managing to get by?'

'Workin' at Mill,' said Sarah. 'I'll point 'er out to you when as I set eyes on 'er. She's only livin' a few doors down from Fred anyhow. Odd sort o' set-up. Mebbe she couldna stand 'is mam. Two women sharin' a kitchen. Dunna allus work.'

'We manage alright,' said Diana with a shrug.

'Not sharin' a man as well, though, are we?' Sarah smiled without humour.

'Seemed a kindly sort of fellow,' said Eliza. 'Not the sort as would be cruel to a woman. Though you can't always tell.' And a thought struck her. 'You don't think he could be the one who gave the lads that cart, do you?'

'S'pose it could a been,' said Sarah. 'Might find out one day, yer never know.'

The boys were reluctant to leave, but were lured away by being reminded of the train journey to come. That, the two older ones enjoyed as much as the earlier journey. Will was worn out and fell asleep in the train and was so floppy and grumpy that he had to be carried most of the way back from the station. Blessedly the sleet had stopped falling, but the temperature had plummeted to a numbness. It was with a feeling of relief that they tumbled into the cottage in Butts Yard.

Boys were unpeeled of wetness. Women the same; and garments were hung regardless of nicety, but wherever they might best relieve themselves of moisture.

Food had to be put together, however tired they were. But first the fire had to be fed and blown and stirred into flame. The kettle, living mostly just aside from the main heat of it, was transferred to the hottest part, whereupon it at last began to bubble. Tea, blessed tea, was made. A pork pie, not the monster that the boys had gazed at, true, but one of more modest proportions, was divided between them. Hunks of bread were held towards the flames. Dripping was applied. Apples, some of the last of the keepers, were bitten into. Peace settled onto the small tribe.

Last of all a rushlight was lit, pincered at an angle in its metal stand, Joe put in charge of looking to its adjustment. It was of the longer and more substantial kind; and might, with luck, last half an hour or so.

Eliza removed her shoes, which needed mending and into which the icy wet of the day had crept, and felt the warm softness of the rag rug beneath her stockings; and was content.

The rug was perhaps not perfect, could be improved upon, would be improved upon. She felt too tired tonight but, and maybe tomorrow, they would start on a new rug. And that one, they having learned from their mistakes, would be even more fine. A rug, however ill-made, certainly insulated against the cold of the beaten-earth kitchen floor.

From outside came the shouts of revellers spilling out of the *Prince of Wales*: Spondon had its share of roisterers who spent more than they should on indulging themselves, to the detriment of wives and children. It was, though, a joyous sound; and Eliza did not begrudge them their Christmas bonhomie.

They woke up to Christmas Eve, which had set itself this year into a Sunday, and thus to a whole day of no work, or rather, no mill-work. It was a splendid feeling, especially as they took note of the weather. Gone was the gloom and wet of the previous day. On each window was a picture of some enchanted land, encrusted in white. You could stare and see ferns, castles, seascapes, whatever your imagination could furnish. Outside, hard frost sparkled underfoot, clung to every branch.

'Let's go skating. Please, please, can we go skating?' It was Jesse.

The women looked at one another. 'When we've done the chores. And you must help. The floors need a good brush. And when we've been to Chapel. Then you can go. You'll 'ave to come back an' change, mind. Not goin' skatin' in your Sunday best.'

The boys jumped up and down. Will scowled and said, 'An' me.'

'We might take you later,' said his mother. You're too young to go just with the boys.'

'An' you pair be careful,' said their mother severely. 'Ice'll only be thin as thin yet, even supposing there is any. We don't want you drowning. Keep to't Lees Brook where it's spilled o'er onto't grass an' don't you be goin' anywhere else. You hear?'

'Where else could they go?' asked Diana, when the boys were out of the way.

'There's down near't station. Derwent floods there onto't fields. That's the favoured place. Trouble is, yer could stray onto't river without meaning to, an' drown. Or there's yon cut, runs by't river. That ices up some years. You could skate all the way from't Trent an' Mersey to't Erewash on that. If you wanted, an' if as barges 'adn't broke it up first, an' if it were cold enough, God forbid. Today they'll be likely just treadin' on't stuff, if it's there at all, an' it cracklin' to bits under 'em.

'Then there's lake at Locko Park,' Sarah went on. 'That's start o't Lees Brook. S'pose it fills lake first, then runs out of it. Must be a spring to start with. Dunno 'ow deep it is, but that ice'll not be anythin' like proper thick enough for days to come. If it keeps on freezin', that is. An' who knows? 'Sides, it's private and they'd be less than welcome. If they was spotted, that is.'

'Have we seen it?'

'That day in September, when we went lookin' for blackberries, we went near. Big 'ouse is further over. Grand 'ouse it is, biggest in Spondon by a long chalk. Dunno 'ow many rooms as there'd be. Family as lives there, they're the Drury-Lowes. Very grand, they are; sort as were born in Paris or London an' 'ave a coachman an' a governess an' nursery-maids an' man-servants an' that. They only live there some o't time 'cos they go off to grand 'ouses in other places besides.'

'All right for some,' said Eliza.

'Before the 'ouse were built,' said Sarah, 'an' long ago, they say as there was an 'ospital there, for lepers. Monks lived there, specially to look after 'em. They tied up their sores wi' rags. An' the rags were called 'loques'. It's French. That's why it's 'Locko', see? Rags Park. Dunna sound quite same, do it?

'Think as the 'ospital got burnt down, though. In't Great Fire o' Spondon, along wi' everything else. Though come to think, that fire must've 'ad to burn for a good mile-an'-an-'alf fore it got to't 'ospital. Probably more woods then, though. An' it must've been a dry bit o' year. And they do say there was a great wind at time, like.'

'So how did it start,' asked Eliza, 'the Great Fire?'

'Well, you must a passed *Malt Shovel*? Yes, course you 'ave. When we goes down 'All Dyke an' then turns right to get to Church Street where me dad lives, that bit o' turning right is Potter Street; an' pub in it, that's *Malt*

Shovel. Course, it ain't the same building exactly, 'cos first one were't first place as burned down.

'It were all on account of they brewed their own beer. Barley 'as to be dried, you know, to make malt; an' someone got fire too 'ot, or they went off an' left it, maybe. Anyway, barley caught fire an' then't malt-'ouse an' then't *Malt Shovel* as were attached to it, an' then't Church and then everything else an' all. Four 'ouses left, there were, them on't side away from't wind.

'They 'ad to send to't King, wring their 'ands an' wail a lot; an' ask him if as 'e'd be a right good bloke an' let 'em off paying taxes while they built the place up again.'

'And did he?' asked Diana, who was absently squishing silverfish as they appeared from impossibly minute cracks.

'Give 'em nine months off,' said Sarah. 'Meant as they 'ad enough pennies to do the rebuilding.'

Coming out of Chapel, where carols had been lustily sung, candles glowed and greenery hung in every possible place, they were intercepted by Martha's mother.

"Ope as you'll not be too put out,' she said, 'but our Martha's turned twelve an's got a post as scullery maid an' she won't be able to look after your boys no more.'

There was silence for a moment. Martha had proved a useful and reliable person. They would have to find a replacement and there was not much time.

'Martha's sister'd be willin'. If you'd 'ave 'er, like. Mary-Jane. 'Er's just left school.'

'Is she here?'

Mary-Jane,' shouted the mother and a slight, dark-haired girl came running over, all legs and elbows.

'Spitting image of young Martha, she is,' said Diana.

'Well, if she's as good as Martha, she'll do,' decided Eliza. So it was all arranged. Mary-Jane would be in Butts Yard at a quarter past six sharp on the Wednesday morning.

Joe and Jesse, socks already drooped around the tops of their oversize Sunday boots, oversize to allow for growth until they became everyday boots, were champing to be gone. When their mother gave them leave they set off at a pace for home, eager to change out of their best. The women followed more slowly, while Will, having been persuaded with difficulty to leave his cart parked at home, and now anxious to rejoin it, galloped after them.

'Soon be able to leave 'em to fend for theirsens,' said Sarah. 'Another year an' Joe'll be eight an' Jesse seven.'

'An' no sign of your Joseph?'

'No sign, ' Sarah said. 'Was askin' Thomas at *Prince o' Wales* yesterday. Nor hide nor hair.'

'He'd never have just left you. He seemed so fond of you. Look how he arranged that hot water, and the house so nice and the piano and all.'

Eliza's heart went out to her friend. Sarah never ranted or moaned or even wept, as far as Eliza knew, but it must be so hard to not know, to not know if you had been abandoned as of no account and left to struggle your own path through the thorny world, to not know whether your husband was alive or dead. She put a consoling arm around her friend and Sarah let it lie.

Christmas Day arrived. The sparkling frost had gone. Fog descended in a murky pall on dirty streets. They stayed indoors, fed heartily, dozed, played Blind Man's Buff and Spin the Platter with the boys, sent Joe round to the *Prince of Wales* with a large jug and sang the old songs.

'One day,' said Diana dreamily, 'I shall have a piano of my own an' we'll all stand round an' sing the very latest tunes.'

Then Boxing Day, one of those blessed St Lubbock's Days, before work reclaimed them. Christmas Day had revivified them. There would likely be a hunt, said Sarah. The South Notts, she said. So they walked into the byways and heard a horn and saw a sandy fox come racing like a streak over the fields with a pack of hounds behind. And after them, rising over hedges in a cloud, a rabble of men in red and four legs under them. Galloping, thudding they came. And the one lone fox was overtaken and disappeared under a seethe of baying hounds.

'They're vermin,' said Sarah.

In the afternoon they made a round of Sarah's relatives, calling first on brother Charlie and his wife Hannah in Butts Yard. A medley of uncles, aunts and cousins came next, a bewildering number of people with whom Eliza and Diana were still only half-acquainted. Those visits were followed by another, to brother William and his wife Sarah on Church Hill where, Eliza was relieved to note, the retiring and melancholy Adolphus of her memory was engaged in a giggling wrestling match with his adoptive brother Will.

The finale was a short further walk to Church Street to see Sarah's father. By this time, they had drunk so much tea and disposed of so many edible offerings that the adults were, as Diana put it, 'fit to burst'. The boys, being boys, had limitless stomachs.

As they came through the door, they saw three lads on the floor playing armies with a couple of dozen lead soldiers. Joe and Jesse drew together: the boys were older than themselves. At school they were seniors, big boys, to be respected and treated with caution.

'Now, John, 'Arry, Joe,' said their father, 'Show young Joe an' Jesse 'ere what you got. Got 'em for Christmas,' he said, turning to the newcomers. 'Leastways, 'Arry an' Joe did. John thinks 'e's a bit above that sort o' thing. Dunna stop 'im playin' with 'em though. Present from Bert 'ere. Though why 'e throws 'is money away on them no-good lads I'll never know.'

Bert was sitting in the second armchair, watching his half-brothers with contentment. Eliza looked at him. So, this was the reclusive brother, the one who couldn't read or write, the one she had not yet met.

His face was florid. His ears winged away from his head. His hair, though thick, had distanced itself unbecomingly from the ears by the use, Eliza thought, of too small a basin. He was on the side of short for a fellow, though probably much the same height as herself.

He stood up without speaking, flushing an even brighter red, and they shook hands.

'An' you lads, good Christmas, was it?' He spoke to the young visitors. But they were already absorbed in watching the soldiers being felled, accompanied by exuberant gun-noises; and hardly responded apart from nods of the head. There was no help there. He stood awkwardly.

'Did you see Rose married off?' Sarah asked her father,

who was now on his knees, placing a few fresh coals judiciously onto the fire.

'That I did. Quiet, like, it were. But I reckons as she's got a good un there. Be looked after, she will.'

'Did you give 'er me gift?'

'I did that, an' she thanks you kindly.'

Will was peering from behind Eliza's skirts.

'An' how's you, young feller-me-lad?' Bert swooped Will off his feet and swung him up onto his shoulders. Will looked first startled, then triumphant, to be at such a height. He clasped Bert's head between his two hands.

Then Bert swung him down and fetched some wooden blocks from a cupboard and began to build them into a tower. The tower grew until it began to totter. Bert touched it gently and, with a tumble and clatter, it fell. Will bent down, picked up a brick and placed it on top of another. The tower grew, but all askew; and soon fell. Eliza looked at her son and at Bert, who seemed as happy as the two-year-old. He was a kindly sort of a chap, she thought.

She felt comfortable: they were becoming accepted in this small and friendly place.

On the Wednesday, Thursday, Friday and the usual half of Saturday, they were back at the Mill. But fortune favoured them this year, for then came Sunday, always a holiday, followed by the first day of 1883, one of those most blessed Bank Holidays.

After that it was all over and the everyday world began again. In the evenings, utilising the short gap between getting a meal together after coming home from the Mill and sleeping, the women would often work on the next rag rug, or knit socks, mittens, scarves and such, by fire-flame and a rushlight. Old knitted garments, fallen into holes or matted by washing or too small because their owners had grown, could be unwound; a spare boy, his hands held apart, acting as a skein-holder. The Queen herself, the black-clad Widow of Windsor, knitted, they knew; although as Diana remarked, she probably did not have to unravel old, knitted chest-protectors or drawers or combinations first. They giggled at the thought, shocked at their irreverence.

At the Mill, people spoke of an astonishing invention. In Derby, a person in an office of the Midland Railway could now be heard in another office or workshop, simply by picking up an instrument known as a telephone and talking into it. The Derby firm of Peters could talk to their branch factory at Borrowash, three whole miles away and be heard as clearly as if they were in the same room. Everyone was familiar with the electric telegraph: it was not entirely unknown for people, even mill-hands like themselves, to have received telegrams. But those were written communications, delivered by a boy trudging out from the post-office: this was one voice speaking directly to another. It was the march of progress.

A funeral was held in the village, which loosed the memories of old people. Mr George Burton, of Church Hill, who had reached his eighty-second year, had once been body-servant to Admiral Anson. He had, long ago, as a lad of thirteen, sailed on the *Northumberland*, a ship bound for a small island named St. Helena and carrying a most important passenger. Mr Burton had told many a

163

story of this voyage; of how for instance the important passenger, recently defeated in a great battle, had played much chess to pass the time and, though he played rather badly, no-one else ever cared to win against him. The important passenger's nickname was Old Boney; and after the sixty-seven days of the voyage, they had left him on the island from which he was never to return. 'And good riddance,' some said.

A bunch of snowdrops was found on the doorstep one Saturday evening while the dark was still falling early. The bunch was tied with a wisp of straw.

Mr Woolley, Fred, as he said to call him, paid the house in Butts Yard a visit. Diana invited him in, where he stood awkwardly, cap in hand.

'Sit thee down,' she implored him. 'The others'll be here any minute.'

"Nay, me duck. I s'll come back another time. Dunna want to be no bother.' And he retreated through the door, re-planting his outsize cap firmly on his head as he went.

Diana gazed after his retreating back, thinking vaguely that his clothes looked more like a Sunday's outfit than one for a Saturday.

'I'll go an' call on 'is mam,' was Sarah's response on being told of the happening. 'Mebbe she'll know as what 'e wanted.'

But Fred's mam knew nothing of it; and Fred himself was out.

A Victorian Miss

11
1883
THE SUITORS

The sun rarely entered Butts Yard, so that as the year advanced it was a pleasure in the early mornings to come out of the dark enclave into the sunshine of their walk to work: something to lift the soul, with the white blossom on the dark tracery of the blackthorn and the tender green of new leaves on the willows and the warmth on your face.

They were familiar with many of their fellow-travellers by now and, within the body, all on the move, gossip scattered, was gathered, embroidered and passed on. To live in Spondon was like living in a very large family, Eliza thought: everyone, even the tiny minority of rank newcomers like herself, Diana and Will, was related to or intimately knew, someone who in their turn was kith or kin to whomever of Spondon's two-thousand inhabitants you chose to be speaking of.

This did mean you had to tread with care. You might, for instance, speak disparagingly of some grasping and snappish shopkeeper who'd short-changed you, only to find that she was your confidante's father's aunt-by-marriage, to be defended to the death and, however belittled within, to be held up to anybody outside the clan as dearly beloved and the very soul of piety and goodness. Repairs had to be effected with rapid skill.

One girl told her that the inhabitants of other towns insulted Spondonians by calling them 'moonrakers'.

'Why?' asked Eliza, wonderingly.

'It means they think people in Spondon are so daft as they'd try to fish reflection of a moon out o't cut, thinkin' it were't real moon, like.'

Eliza remembered a story of her mother's, something similar. 'In the story I heard,' she said, 'they weren't so daft after all. They were smugglers an' they'd hidden bottles of whisky in the village pond. They were trying to fish 'em out with a net when a party of soldiers arrived an' wanted to know what they were doing. So one says, "We was just fishin' out that great big yellow cheese there, Sir." An' the soldiers near killed themselves laughing an' left the simpletons to it.'

'Reckon that's more like the men o' Spondon,' another girl said, as they all smiled.

Eliza had a letter from Sarah-Ann, one of her sister's increasingly rare missives. Sarah-Ann had had a letter from their father, who had asked after his grandson. He had grumbled about his name: 'William' was an unlucky name, he'd said.

'At least he acknowledges he's *got* a grandson,' thought

Eliza. She supposed he had taken offence at the boy not being called John after himself. 'And he might have been, if he hadn't turned me out.'

The letter said their father was doing well, making money. His stepson George had joined Frank in working for him and he was set up in his own business as builder and contractor. They employed a household servant. He'd like to see Diana sometime.

Sarah-Ann did not mention her own children. William, her husband, had changed jobs again. She feared him being out of work. There was so much left unsaid, thought Eliza. She wished she could speak to her sister, wished she were nearer. The telephone came to mind: no hope of that, more's the pity. She foraged for pen and paper, borrowed a doubtful-looking pot of ink and wrote a reply, the nib crossing and spluttering the page. Could her sister persuade William to come to Spondon? There was work, for both men and women; and rents were not too high.

Alfred Woolley came calling again, one Sunday after Chapel, bearing a rabbit, fresh skinned, gutted and ready for the pot. 'Ah've a friend,' he said, 'as can lay 'is 'and on a rabbit from time to time …' And no-one asked him for further details, but relieved him of the creature with small cries of pleasure. He seemed more certain of himself after that and was made to sit down before the fire and accept a cup of tea and a griddle-cake, the mixture made up by Diana that very morning for use later. And now, here one was, its scent making the taste-buds quiver, its heat melting the butter.

Fred savoured it - they could see him doing so - scraping up the runny overflow with a horny forefinger.

'Would you care for another?' asked Diana in her best hostess voice, while their guest accepted and they watched their own treat dwindling away.

'Well, what dost think '*e* came for?' Sarah questioned when their visitor had taken his leave.

'Don't know,' said Eliza, 'But I'll bet he'll be back. Even if it's only for another griddle-cake.'

'I reckon a few griddle-cakes aren't a bad exchange for a rabbit,' said Diana. 'Though he did go heavy on our bit of butter.'

'I remember where thyme grows wild,' Sarah said. 'It's not too far. Let's go an' find some before it gets dark. We can put this 'ere rabbit on to seethe slow like, an' put in the thyme when we gets back. If we takes the boys, they'll learn where it is an' what it is, an' we can just send 'em next time we wants some.'

So off they set, with Joe and Jesse and Will, finding the plant in a close-cropped pasture. Coming back, they spotted new watercress in the brook and took it for spoils, along with chickweed and dandelion leaves.

Sarah also noted a thick crop of nettles: 'Catch 'em young, like these, make lovely soup wi' a bit o' broth,' she said. 'Like as we'll have over from't rabbit. But we s'll leave 'em for now, as we'll need gloves; an' best have a knife to cut. Them nettles, they've a rare sting on 'em. An' you needs a fair few, they goes down so. Clean the blood an' all, they do. An' a fair few other things. Better than Cockle's Pills. And cheaper.'

Neither Eliza nor Diana had come across nettle soup.

'We've always lived in towns,' Diana said. 'You only learn about shops there. An' nothing grew in Ancoats. Not even the people,' she added.

Eliza thought that was true enough: people in Spondon looked more healthy, seemed on the whole more robust, taller, than those who had endured since birth the grimy wastes of Ancoats.

A bunch of pale primroses was found, laid in the corner of the front doorstep. Diana put them in water in a jar.

'People used to make wine from't flowers,' said Sarah. 'Still do, probably. If you know where there's enough of 'em.'

Fred was seen one Sunday where not normally to be found, in Chapel; and greeted them heartily on the way out.

'Is he still married?' Eliza asked.

'Aye,' said Sarah. 'An' 'is wife still livin' a few doors down. Doubt she's comin' back after all this time. Doubt Joseph will neither.'

One morning the gossips, walking to work, were sombre. There were shakings of heads, shakings against belief, mouths drawn down.

'What's up?' asked Sarah.

A girl answered. 'It's Will Tomlinson. Works at Colour Works. They say as 'e were by 'is machine an' summat got stuck like, so 'e pokes it wi' a stick an't stick gets stuck, so 'e tries to get it out an' is arm gets drawed into't rollers. They turns machine off but 'is arm's been pulled clean out on 'is shoulder. So they gets 'im to the Derby Infirmary, but 'e's dead like. Worked in the ware'us really, but 'e'd been told to take over the machine. First time on't job. Only nineteen, 'e was. Poor Will.'

None of them could quite bring to mind Will Tomlinson. But his death cast a shadow over the May day: each of Sarah's three brothers worked at Leach and Neal's Colour Works.

The claim by William Tomlinson's father for the loss of a son, a claim for compensation of three year's work at sixteen shillings a week, the maximum allowed under the recent Employers' Liability Act, was disallowed by the Judge. A lack of safety precautions, His Honour ruled, did not equate to a defect of equipment and did not therefore come within the Act. No compensation could be paid.

It was at this May time, days of lengthening light and warmth, when green had crept over raw brown earth and flourished over hedge and tree, waxing into lush beauty, that Eliza felt most lonely. There was a longing in her, an incompleteness. She thought of Fred Woolley. Did he feel this too? And which of the three women drew him to the house in Butts Yard?

She reminded herself that he was a married man, in the eyes of the Church and of the law; and thus not free to do as he wanted. Nor should any self-respecting woman cast her eyes on him. Though he was, again, very good-looking.

Sarah, through her grapevine of relatives and acquaintances, was the mother-lode of local news. She sometimes, and even more often of late, left the other two on the way home from work, coming in when they had all long eaten. She had been visiting, she said, and would regale them with gossip about the villagers.

A man had died, she told them one night, hit by a train on the railway near the station: quite sober he was too, the inquest was told. Another was fined for obstructing the highway with a cart. There were several cases of being drunk and disorderly, one most reprehensibly female. A horse and trap was stolen, likewise some apples, and a hundred weight and a half of iron from the brickyard. Someone was fined for riding a bicycle on the footpath; and two men for flirting stones at the telegraph posts. Ten lads were hauled up before the magistrates at Derby, charged with playing a game of chance - pitch and toss - in the public highway at Spondon. Two of them were Cope lads and were fined the enormous sum of 2s.6d each, plus costs.

One evening she was full of talk of a chap whose renown had spread further than Spondon.

'You might've seen 'im,' she said. 'When us first came. George Porter. Livin' in Chapel Street then. Big feller, well set-up, flat cap, moustache. Proper cricketer 'im. Professional. Played for South Derbyshire, though 'e's playin' for Wigan now. They say 'e's doing really well for 'is self. Started off as a chimney sweep, apprenticed to 'is uncle, like. Bit of a change, black from 'ead to toe, to all in white.'

One evening, as the days grew even longer, a knock came at the door. They were not expecting anyone. Sarah shrugged and went to open it. It was her brother.

'Come in, Bert. Taken thee long enough to visit us. Cup o' tea while you're 'ere?'

Diana pushed the kettle over the flames. It was the

smallest of fires, being June: but if you had no fire, there was no means of cooking. Bert sat down, looking ill at ease. Then he fished in his pocket and brought out three wooden objects. He put one to his mouth and blew. His fingers moved over the stem. Notes came out, a tune. He handed one to each of the boys who had stopped what they were doing to watch him.

'See them 'oles? Now, stop all o' them wi' your fingers. Like this ... Now, blow. Gently now. Keep blowin'. Take off one finger ... '

The boys tried; came a medley of odd noises. They persevered.

'Good, mind you keep practisin',' said Bert, satisfied. He accepted his tea.

They made halting conversation, which came more easily as time passed. He relaxed enough to look around him, and, as his sister looked at him in astonishment, admired their rug. They had the third attempt under their feet now, the first two banished to the bedrooms. Diana sliced up some cold potatoes, put a lump of dripping in a pan; and they heard a sputtering, watched the ovals browning at the edges, smelt the savour of them, ate them with their fingers, passing them from one hand to another until they cooled enough to eat.

Sarah teased him, scolding him for being up so late. 'An' you only a young 'un,' she said.

Eliza liked him. True, he was not the most handsome of men, but he was kindly. And his talk was interesting now he had relaxed. And it was good of him to think of the boys.

Before he went, he turned to Eliza. 'Mrs Kirby,' he began, his face even redder than usual, 'I 'opes as you'll not think it forrard of me, but mebbe after work next Saturday, you an' Will'll come wi' me to watch't cricket? An' Miss Diana, o' course,' he went on, turning towards her. And, in afterthought, 'An' me sister.'

Eliza had a moment of surprise. Then, 'That's very kind of you, Mr Cope. I'm sure Will'd love to. Wouldn't you, Will?'

Will, who by now had put the pipe into his cart and was pulling it round the room, nodded.

'Well, better be off,' said Bert, getting to his feet. Diana handed him his cap. And as he positioned it on his head, Eliza caught a flash of blue tucked into the lining. It was a wing feather.

'Well,' said Sarah, 'You've made a conquest there, young Eliza. Never would a thought I'd see our Bert lookin' at a woman. Allus kept 'imself to 'imself 'as our Bert. Well, mostly. Bit choosy, 'im. But 'e's a good un, though I says it meself. An 'ard worker is our Bert, an' straight as a die. You go an' watch cricket. Cricket's big in Spondon. Dost know about cricket?'

Eliza gave a wry grin, 'It's a game,' she said. 'There's a bat an' a ball an' they wear white an' run about an' it goes on for a long, long time.'

'Well, you'll be able to ask a lot o' questions, then, won't you? Nothin' a man likes more than bein' able to answer a whole lot o' questions. Makes 'em feel important like.'

Saturday arrived. They returned from the mill and had a quick bite to eat. Eliza tidied herself up, changed her clogs for shoes, put on her better shawl and her Sunday bonnet, the one with the feather in it. On further thought she removed the feather. Then she fetched Will and tidied him up too, brushing his hair and pulling up his ever-drooping socks.

She felt nervous. 'Don't be so daft,' she told herself. 'He's harmless. But whatever shall we talk about? Cricket, you stupid woman. Anyway, you won't be on your own, there's plenty of others to help out.'

Bert called and they walked in convoy to the ground. It wasn't far, but then nothing was far in Spondon. Others converged: it was the fairest of summer days, cricket was popular, and excitements were few.

They found what Bert deemed to be a position of advantage and prepared to sit on the sheep-nibbled grass. Eliza found a jacket whipped off and placed under her to protect her from the gifts that sheep are wont to scatter behind them. She thanked her protector, feeling rather singled out and hoped aloud that his jacket would not be damaged. Bert's sister giggled.

'Eh duck, that there jacket's seen a sight worser'n that,' she said.

The game had long begun. Eliza looked around the ground. Hedges formed a rough boundary; men, most wearing at least something white, some half-crouched, all with intent stance, were dotted around the space. A man walked some distance, turned, threw the ball with force towards another man standing slightly hunched, bat in hand, before three wooden sticks with another over them. The ball evaded the bat and the sticks fell. Players and spectators let out a mighty cry. Clapping ensued, in which Eliza joined, though the exact nature of the triumph eluded her. Herbert was ecstatic.

A Victorian Miss

The man with the bat left the sticks and walked off the field, crossing the path of another man who took his former place. A few more balls were forcefully hurled. Sometimes the men - for Eliza had realised that another man stood at the far end of the strip - ran towards each other and past, turned and charged back again. Once a man hit a ball far into the air, which was intercepted by a desperado who leapt high, caught it in one hand and rolled on the ground with it, to fierce clapping and shouts of appreciation from the audience. Well, it was a lovely day, thought Eliza, closing her eyes and giving herself up to the warmth of the sun and the atmosphere of cheer and applause.

Diana was pestering Bert with innumerable questions.

Through her half-consciousness, Eliza gathered that Spondon was playing a village named Mickleover; and after a long, long time, that Mickleover had scored thirty-six, while Spondon had seventy-seven. She woke up and looked enthusiastic with the rest. Herbert was grinning with satisfaction. He looked towards her hopefully.

'A right good game, that,' he said. 'Didst enjoy it?'

She smiled. 'I enjoyed it very much,' she said.

The Band of Hope visited Spondon. Spondon, it was regretfully put about, had been failing in its observance of temperance. A public tea was held, after which a person of importance, no less than the Minister of King Street Chapel, Derby, gave a rousing address devoted to the dangers of intoxicants. Sankey's stirring melodies were sung to the accompaniment of a harmonium. A well-scrubbed, insipid-looking man gave a moving account of his conversion from sinner to saint.

The meeting drew to a successful conclusion: twenty children vowed never to indulge in spirituous liquors and a handful of old people renewed their pledges.

Sadly, the little group from Butts Yard were unable to attend and learnt of the meeting through gossip only.

"Ast ever been to Matlock?' It was Bert, addressing Eliza one August day.

She shook her head. 'Where is it?'

'On't way from Derby to Buxton - an' that's another place as you mun see.'

'I think we might've come through it when we came down from Manchester,' Eliza said. She was much more at ease with Bert now, and he with her, which was a relief. She liked him: he was always kind to Will and the other two boys.

'Then us'll go,' said Bert. 'Just you an' me an' Will. There's a train, excursion train, leaves Derby five past two of a Saturday afternoon, catch it back late, nine twenty-five. Sunday the next day, naught to fret about.'

It was exciting to think of an excursion, on a special train, laid on for the purpose. The girls at the mill went on them sometimes. Some had been as far as the Isle of Man, or Brighton, or Scarborough 'the Queen of Watering Places', even London.

The day dawned at last. Work until midday of course. Will was at Spondon station, waiting under the supervision of his minder, Mary-Jane. How much longer would she be with them, Eliza wondered, before, like her sister, she moved on to women's work?

Eliza surveyed her son. He was two and a half, full of

unfocused energy. Mary-Jane had brushed his hair, which was silky and straight, fairish now, but would probably darken to match his brown eyes; and she had brushed his dress, over which he wore a clean pinafore. He broke into a smile as he saw his mother.

'Train,' he said. 'Will wants train.' He jumped up and down.

'We've seen one just now,' said Mary-Jane, reprovingly.

'Will want more trains.' He scowled.

'Well, you'll be on one in a minute,' said Mary-Jane. She gave his bottom a little pat.

'Any sign of Mr Cope?' asked Eliza, anxiously.

He hove into sight, walking quickly, jingling coins in his hand. 'Let's get us tickets, quick, afore't train comes.'

They went into the booking office, all polished wood and marble floor, with the clerk behind a glass window taking his ponderous time.

Then the train was approaching, an excitement that never failed to lift your heart. It hissed to a stop, doors banged open, they climbed in. A whistle blew, a flag waved. They were off, a waving Mary Jane growing smaller by the moment.

Eliza gazed through the window, Will on her lap, pointing out sights to her son. In no time they were in Derby, changing trains, going north, stopping at every station, through a tunnel, past crops and cattle; flat land giving way to steep wooded hillsides, the river appearing and disappearing.

'Next station,' said Bert. He seemed confident of the way. 'Matlock Bath.'

The train slowed, drew to a halt. They descended, Bert

first, helping Eliza down the steep step from train to platform.

Here they were, at the bottom of a valley with the river snaking beside them.

'Derwent,' said Bert. 'Same as near us. Can't get away from it, can us?'

'It's a lovely river,' said Eliza. 'Will! No!' raising her hands in alarm as he made a dash for the water's edge.

Bert scooped him up. 'We'll cross over to t'other side on't ferry,' he said. 'That's where't main street is an' we can get us a bite to eat.'

They found a stall selling pies and sat outside to enjoy them. Eliza looked around her. On the far side of the narrow gorge a bare, white cliff rose through the tangle of greenery. Their side was steep too, though richly covered in trees; and houses had somehow found purchase there, like nesting birds. There were large, imposing buildings besides: hotels, Bert told her.

'Little Switzerland, they calls it,' said Bert.

The street where they sat was lined on one side with solid stone buildings, many of them shops. The concourse was crowded; ladies there were, some with parasols against the sun, men in striped blazers and panama hats. Vehicles edged their way through the crowd. They sat and gazed out over the river, too deep just here for Will to paddle. It was soothing to sit there in the sun and do not much at all, just look and rest.

'When you're ready,' said Bert, 'We'll walk along by't river. We can go upstream and we can go down. North Parade or South Parade.'

'Which way shall we go, Will?' Eliza asked. Will pointed. They got up and began to stroll. One shop was a jewellers', displaying riches Eliza had seen only in the most celebrated shops of Manchester.

'It's the Spas,' said Bert. 'Folks've come to take waters 'ere for 'undreds o' years. An' they're rich folk, wi' plenty o' time to think about 'ow ill they are, an' plenty o' money to 'ave an 'oliday to cure it. An' then other folks, folks wi' a bit o' nous, says, 'Best give 'em summat to look at while they're stuck out 'ere, an' summat to buy besides.'

They walked on, gazing at gowns imported from London and Paris, tobacco pipes of every shape and size, eight-day clocks and coral necklets.

'They turns things to stone 'ere,' said Bert. 'Folks used to think it were magic, or witchcraft.'

'Oh, can we see?'

'In 'ere.' They had come to a building advertising itself as the Royal Museum Petrifying Well. They gazed in awe at stone hats, a stone basket containing stone eggs, a gentleman's curled wig rigid in stone, hundreds of objects.

'It's special water, see. Looks like magic, though.'

They visited a cavern. In the dark, Bert kissed her. It was a good kiss, firm, dry, giving. It was the kiss of a man who knows what he's about, thought Eliza. Her blood responded.

Will stumbled in front of them, cries of pain. He had to be caught up, soothed. When they walked on, Bert put his arm around her waist. She did not move it away. But there was an urgency, a shame. She must tell him. She waited, putting off the moment, savouring the protectiveness of the arm, the feel of his body close against her own. She drowsed in bliss.

They came out into sunlight again. She moved away

from his encircling arm.

'Bert,' she said. ' I've got to tell you something.' She stopped. He faced her, looking directly at her, expectant.

'Bert,' she said. 'I'm not a widow-woman. I never was married.' She stopped, waiting, lowered her head.

What she got was a return of an arm around her. He turned her to face him; and in broad daylight he kissed her once more. 'I knows as you're not,' he said. 'Leastways, I suspected as you wasn't. Don't matter, not to me. Would you 'ave a man as can't read nor write? That's more important. Canst like a man 'o's just an ornary feller, an' none too 'andsome at that, while you's the cleverest, prettiest, dearest girl in all of the world?

12
1883
AN UNEXPECTED VISITOR

They were walking out. It was understood. Eliza found a new flow of interest towards her. Men she had hitherto failed to notice tipped their caps as she walked by. She enjoyed the sensation: a small glow of importance crept into her.

She remembered her father, black-browed, grizzle-bearded, his grim words the day he threw her out: 'You'll never be nothin' now! Never! Go to the gutter where you belongs!' He had been in a fury such as she'd never witnessed before, names like slut and whore spraying at her.

It had knifed deep, that contumely: she'd never quite dared to hope that she could ever again be respectable. And now, here was this chance it seemed. She felt she could dance. Could Bert dance? She grinned. Probably not, though you never knew. They might try sometime, nobody watching, of course.

A sound ... Was that a knock? She went to the door. Her eyes fell on a figure propping itself upright against the doorpost, wrapped in rags, thin, bonnet-less, hair in greasy strings; and wild, huge eyes in a bony face. It spoke.

'Eliza?'

She stared at the creature and with a sense of shock saw her sister, Sarah-Ann. What terrifying event had plucked her from her family and cast her up here?

She put out her arm, reached for her and drew her in. She guided the apparition into the back room and sat it in a chair. She pushed the kettle over the fire till it began to sing. She dashed upstairs for a blanket to wrap the gaunt frame. She made a fresh pot of tea. She drew out bread and milk and cheese and jam, anything she could lay hands upon. She eased off the terrible shoes. And all the while she was making soothing noises and exclamations of sorrow and comforting noises, hardly aware of what she was about.

She warmed milk, dropped into it pieces of torn bread, sprinkled precious sugar over and fed her sister with a spoon. Sarah-Ann ate. And it seemed as if she would never stop.

It was so fortunate she'd not gone to Chapel that morning: a heavy cold. The others had thought she would be better off staying at home and she had been happy to have it that way.

She took her sister's two hands in hers. Dirty hands, thin hands, on scrawny arms. She stank: of unwashed clothes, of filth and sweat.

'Sarah-Ann, oh, Sarah-Ann, why ... how ... why ...? Oh, what's happened? Where's William, where's Eliza-Ann? Where's the baby? Why aren't you in Ardwick? What's happened? Why're you here? How did you get here? How can you be in such a state?'

Sarah-Ann's eyes were full of tears. She drew a torn sleeve across her face, but the sobs began, the tears flowed and she began to keen in anguish.

'I'm sorry, sister. I'm so sorry, so sorry, sorry to bring this on you. But I didn't know what to do. An' I couldn't go on any longer an' I couldn't think of where to go, not anywhere, anywhere, so I came here in the end.'

'But William? Why isn't he looking after you?'

'William, he changed. He began to get funny. Little things it was at first, but it got worse. He said such strange things. I didn't understand. Nobody could understand. He lost his job because he kept shouting at people, saying they'd done things they hadn't, stolen from him, lied about him, and he went about talking to himself and he couldn't keep still, couldn't stay in one place and then he'd be back again, looking for something he could never find and he began to talk to people who weren't there at all. I couldn't see them an' no-one else could neither. And he got worse an' worse and he thought he was a bird who could fly, or a stone, fixed for ever, and he thought he was the Lord ...' she hid her face in her hands ... 'An' he thought I was his enemy an' I was so a-feared.'

'But his parents?'

'They wouldn't believe me at the start of it, then they didn't see him when he was really bad. Somehow he seemed better when he was with them. An' then, when they did see him really bad, they blamed me, said it was my fault an' I was a bad wife an' they'd never wanted him to marry me, not really, an' it was me driven him out of his mind. An' I wanted to go but there was nowhere to go to an' then when I couldn't take no more they said the girls were William's an' I couldn't have them an' I was a bad mother an' they wouldn't let me take them so I just left one night an' ran an' ran, anywhere to get away - we were living with them by then. An' how could we have lived anyway, if as I'd taken them? Me an' two girls an' nowhere to go an' nothing to eat? They'd be better off with them than with me. At least they were kind to the girls.' Tears overcame her.

Eliza stroked her hands, her back, hugged her, rocked with her, crooned baby-talk and comfort.

Then the present came into her mind. The others would be back soon from Chapel. Herbert might come back with them. She recoiled from the idea that his first sight of her sister should be of a woman in such dire straits.

'Sarah,' she said. 'Sarah, I'm going to try an' arrange things. Now, look, you just lie down on the rug in front of the fire, and I'll get some hot water going an' the tub out so as we can clean you up. I've got mebbe half an hour before they're out of Chapel. Then I s'll go up to meet them, say you've come but you're not well. Get Sarah to take the boys round to her dad's maybe. Then Diana an' I can look after you awhile till we've put you to rights a bit.'

Sarah-Ann nodded. Eliza helped her from chair to rug. She could barely stand. How she'd managed to finish her journey, Eliza could only wonder.

Sarah-Ann curled into a ball, shivering. Eliza rushed upstairs, snatched a second blanket, spread it over the exhausted figure. There were lice, she noticed with repulsion. She picked up the discarded shoes, cracked, soles flapping; and saw fresh blood on her sister's feet.

She went outside and lugged the tin bath from the lean-to. She poured water from the small tank next to the range into a pan, transferred it to the bath and replenished the water in the tank. She stoked up the fire - needs must - and hoped the water would not take too long. She re-filled the kettle and what pans they had and put them over the heat.

She found a wide-toothed comb and scissors, for hair and nails. How long had her sister been on the road? How had she eaten? Where had she slept? If she'd come straight here, knowing the route and not gone out of her way, and had she been fit and strong, she could have been here in five days. But she looked as if she had suffered for far longer than that, as if she had been half-starved and neglected for weeks, even months.

Sarah-Ann was sleeping. Eliza looked down at her and thought of her own nights alone on the streets and how terrified and desperate she herself had been; and that was for such a short time. And she thought wryly of William's rescue of herself and of what a hero he had been in her eyes. She'd been fond of him, still was. How could a man change so?

She went out into Chapel Street and saw the first of the congregation leaving, coming towards her. She waited, forcing herself to exchange words with all those people becoming so familiar to her; and blessed her present lot. To think she had once been envious of her sister, respectably married, with a house occupied only by husband, herself and daughter. Life was full of unexpected hazards. You never could tell what perils lay in wait.

Sarah arrived first, with Joe and Jesse racing ahead, twirling to a stop as they met, unexpectedly, Eliza. She barred them from going further, seized the arm of Sarah and told her in as few words as possible what had happened. Sarah, bless her, grasped the situation, motioned to her sons, caught Will by the hand and set off for Church Street, Will dragging, looking back with puzzlement. Diana, left with her sister, gazed after them in mild surprise.

'Come on,' said Eliza and returned to the cottage, filling in the story the while.

Sarah-Ann was still asleep. Eliza woke her, though she resisted; and together the two girls got their sister into the warm water. Eliza soaped her hair, Diana her hands. Piece by piece they worked, combing out her tangled locks, being gentle with the damaged feet.

When they thought her clean enough, they stood her up while Eliza poured a final pan of fresh water over her. They helped her out, rubbed her dry and put an old nightgown of Eliza's, a conversion from a man's cast-off shirt, over her head. Then they supported her up the stairs, laid her down on the rag rug in their room, spread the blankets over her once more; and left her to sleep.

'We'll leave the hair-cutting to another time,' said Eliza. 'If it's needed.'

'Let's get these clothes of hers soaking,' said Diana. So they put those that were rescuable into the tub, including some that could eke out a further life as rags, consigning the rest to the flames.

A Victorian Miss

It was now dinner-time. 'Shall I go and find the others? Most likely they'll still be at Sarah's dad's, I should think,' Diana said.

She went off while Eliza put their meal together.

'We've got Auntie Sarah-Ann upstairs,' Eliza began.

'Auntie Sarah-Ann, Auntie Sarah-Ann,' chanted Will.

'Why's she here?' asked Joe.

'Where'll she sleep?' asked Jesse.

'Want to see Auntie Sarah-Ann,' said Will.

'She's asleep just now,' said Diana.

'Why?' asked Will, who was at that age.

' 'Cause she's very tired,' Eliza answered.

'Why?'

' 'Cause she's come a very long way to see us.'

'Why?'

' 'Cause she 'as. An' them that asks no questions don't get told no lies,' said Sarah firmly. 'Now, come an' get your dinners.'

Talk died for a while in the face of more important things.

Then, as hunger came near to being satisfied, 'Gaffer Douglass gived Joe a good 'iding the other day,' remarked Jesse.

His brother glared. All eyes turned upon him.

'An' what were that for?' his mother asked sternly.

'An' 'e made Joe stand on a chair all morning,' added Jesse, virtuously.

Their mother frowned. 'What'd you done?' she demanded.

187

'I ain't done nothing,' said Joe; and scowled.

'Huh,' said his mother. 'Mr Douglass don't do things like that for nothing. Don't you go doin' it again, do you 'ear? An' don't let me 'ear you callin' 'im 'Gaffer', not neither on you. It's disrespectful. An' I've a good mind to make you go without your rice puddin' an' all.' But she relented.

On Sundays, boys and girls were expected to pursue improving occupations, such as reading the Bible or perhaps, for girls, plain sewing. However, the little group of women in the Butts were not as strict as some and so the boys were released to gather kindling, for which there was a constant need. They had to change out of their Sunday clothes, look after Will most carefully and promise neither to shout nor to run.

'It'll last till they gets to top o't street, mebbe,' said Sarah, resignedly. 'Now, tell us more about Sarah-Ann.'

Eliza began the story, trying to remember every detail. Diana joined in when it came to the part she had played.

'Eh dear.' Sarah shook her head. 'An' 'er 'avin' to leave them children an' all. Must a fair broke 'er 'eart, poor soul.'

'Well, we all live here,' said Eliza, looking from one to another. 'We should all have a say. What should we do?'

'We can't turn 'er away, that's for certain,' said Sarah.

'She'll have to stay,' said Diana. 'We could lend her some clothes. I've got two shawls: she can have one o' those. An' I've got a spare pair of stockings. We're much the same size, now, the three of us.'

'I've got that spare pair of stays,' said Eliza. 'I was going to give them to the rag-and-bone man, but they'd be alright at a pinch for a month or two. She can have those.

Hers went on the fire. Dunno how long she'd been wearing them, all the bones poking through.'

'Shoes,' said Diana. 'There's a problem.'

They contemplated the one remaining shoe, whose fellow was contributing to the warmth of the room.

'There wasn't no mending those,' said Eliza.

'I'll ask around,' said Sarah.

'No, don't do that,' Eliza said. 'Or you might have to do more explaining than's needful.'

'There's the cobbler, shoemaker, 'e calls 'isself, on Moor Street, Mr Elson. 'E'd make 'er a pair.'

They contemplated again. This was not a decision to be taken lightly.

'They'd last,' said Diana hopefully.

'Well, I've not got shoes to spare,' said Eliza. None of them had. Shoes were difficult things to come by and once got, you hung onto them for as long as possible, greasing and polishing, mending till you could mend no more. Some men, good with their hands, managed to get hold of a last and cut their own shapes out of leather and glued or sewed or nailed them on for their household.

'Sometimes 'e 'as second'and shoes in 'is winder,' said Sarah, hopefully. 'Or clogs, even.'

'Clogs aren't half hard on the feet,' said Diana. 'To wear all the time. I'm only really thankful for them in the wet, these days, keeping the water out of my shoes.'

They left the problem to simmer.

'We'll be going to work tomorrow,' said Eliza.

'Well, she can lie in, then get 'ersen used to't place. Then us'll see.'

Sarah-Ann woke about supper-time. Those below

189

heard a movement, a creak of boards followed by a thin voice. Eliza and Diana climbed the stairs. Sarah-Ann was sitting up, blanket clutched around her shoulders. She gave a faint smile before weak tears dripped down.

The two sisters knelt down and hugged her.

'You're safe now,' Diana said.

Sarah-Ann stretched an arm round each of them. 'Thank the Good Lord for sisters.'

They had made a pile of clothing for her, held up each garment one by one; and Diana pretended to be a fawning assistant in a fancy drapery shop, calling Sarah-Ann 'Modom', while pointing out the superiority of each well-used garment and making them all laugh. Sarah-Ann cried while she laughed.

Tension eased, they went downstairs for a meal. There were crumpets and jam and plenty of tea. They gave Sarah-Ann perhaps more than her share, while the three boys, returned from their adventures, looked on.

'She eats a lot,' said Jesse.

'Jesse!' said his mother. 'Go an' stand in't corner! You rude, bad boy.'

They all became silent and awkward.

'Jesse,' said his mother. 'Say sorry to Aunt Sarah-Ann.'

'Sorry, Aunt Sarah-Ann,' Jesse mumbled.

'Aunt Sarah-Ann,' said Eliza, 'has kindly walked a very long way to see us, and she'll be staying for a while. We s'll all make her welcome, 'cause it's polite to help a guest.'

'Why?' asked Will.

'Because,' said Sarah firmly. And that was that.

Herbert didn't get to see Sarah-Ann for a few days; and in the meantime Eliza filled him in, glossing over the exact nature of her brother-in-law's shortcomings, shifting them rather to unreasonable behaviour and sad neglect. To her, William's condition, as portrayed by Sarah-Ann, sounded far more alarming. True, she was sure there could be no hereditary taint, William being not of her blood. But she still didn't know Bert well enough to judge his reaction to the frightening thing she suspected: madness lurked around the lives of some, but it was spoken of in whispers, if at all.

By the time the two met, Bert and Sarah-Ann, her hair was neat, if noticeably less abundant and glossy than in former times; and she was decently, if somewhat poorly, clothed. Some people might have had a puzzled half-knowledge of having seen her garments before.

'Men dunna notice clothes anyways,' said Sarah. 'They just 'as a sort of idea o' the shape inside 'em an' a feeling as they'd like to see more on it.'

Fortunately, due to the reclaimed stays, the shape was passable. And no-one, not even Sarah-Ann, could find fault with a waist that was more slender than it had been for years.

'See,' said Diana, triumphantly, eyeing her sister from all angles by walking round her standing person. 'There's always something good comes out of things, however bad they seem at the time.'

Sarah-Ann even had footwear, bought from Mr Elson's Moor Street emporium. Ladies' Strong Calf Elastics they were, made for hard wear and costing the enormous sum of 3s.9d.

'I've been thinking,' said Sarah-Ann, one evening a couple of weeks later. They looked at her expectantly. It was one of their rag-rug evenings, though Sarah was darning her sons' socks - 'Ow they gets 'oles like this I'll never know. More 'ole than sock, nearly.'

'I can't stay here for ever, an' I don't want to work at the mill, an' I couldn't afford to rent a place on me own even if I did. Think as I'll go into service again. I know about that an' I could live in.'

Sarah considered. 'You'd be lucky to get a place in Spondon,' she said. 'Places do come up from time to time, but they're often spoken for already. You'd be best in a big place like Derby. That way you'd not be far, either.'

There was a silence while this was thought over.

'An' I'm going to Derby meself,' said Sarah, suddenly. They all looked at her in surprise. 'I know, I know, I've said nowt; but Fred an' me, we're both goin'.'

'So that's where you've been,' said Eliza, light dawning, 'All those evenings you said as you were visiting cousins an' such!'

'You're right,' said her friend. 'I can't gainsay it. I allus 'ad a soft spot for Fred. Knowed 'im since 'e were a nipper. An' though 'e were a bit younger'n me - only a couple o' years, mind - now we're older, it don't seem to matter as much, like. An' 'is missis, she don't want 'im back. An' we can't easy stay in Spondon, with 'is missis 'ere, an' all the tongues waggin'. So we thinks it best to go to Derby, where no-one knows us, an' we'll set up together wi' the boys. Fred's 'appy to take the boys, though I knows as some men wouldna.'

They drank this in.

'Well,' said Eliza. 'I'm happy for you, if that's what you want.' Then, 'But what about Joseph?'

'Joseph ain't never comin' back,' said Sarah flatly.

A Victorian Miss

'Whatever 'appened, I know I s'll never see 'im again. If 'e were goin' to come back, 'e'd a come by this time. No-one's 'eard, nor 'ide nor 'air. An' I'm gettin' on, thirty-three; an' it's the best chance as I'll 'ave.'

The four women mulled these revelations over.

'Everything's breaking up,' said Diana. 'It was all so settled and now everything's changed. We were happy. Weren't we?'

Eliza and Sarah nodded.

'It's me,' Sarah-Ann broke in. 'I've spoilt it all, coming here. Upset things, like.'

'Course you haven't,' said Eliza. 'Now don't start blaming yourself. It's got nothing to do with you. More likely it's me, marrying Bert, like.'

'Or me,' said Sarah, 'Goin' off wi' Fred. But I shan't go till you're wed, Liza. Fred's got to find a job, anyhow. 'E'll go first, find a job an' an 'ouse. Then I'll follow wi't boys.'

'In the meantime,' said Diana, 'we s'll feed you up, Sarah-Ann. Feed you till you're fat as a pig, an' then we'll help you look for a situation. "Fat Parlour-maid wanted for Friendly Family. All Found. Generous Wages. Live in."'

'If only,' said Sarah-Ann, but she managed a smile.

13
1883
THE BEST OF TIMES

Will was collecting useful objects in his cart. He would pull it towards an object of suitable size that he had spotted, put the object in the cart and then pull it to another place, explaining to his object-friends the while. So far, he had an empty cotton reel, one knitting needle, a sock without a mate; and a fluff of thistledown which had flown in through the open door and seemed undecided at each moment whether to fly off again. It was a hot Saturday afternoon in August.

The boys, Joe and Jesse, having finished their household jobs, were out somewhere, doing whatever boys did on sunny August afternoons: climbing trees or paddling in brooks perhaps, or playing cricket with a plank for a bat, three sticks in the ground and whatever most nearly approached a cricket ball. Imagination loomed large in these doings.

Mary-Jane had been set free as soon as the women were back from the mill. They still had Mary-Jane. Having a guest in the shape of Sarah-Ann had strained the budget of the cottage in Butts Yard and they had wondered whether to let Mary-Jane go, devolving her nursemaid duties onto Sarah-Ann's shoulders: it would be cheaper. But it was not certain how long Sarah-Ann would be with them; and when she left they would again need a minder. Mary-Jane by then would be unavailable, having found occupation elsewhere; and good Mary-Janes did not grow on every bush: they had been lucky so far, Martha and then Mary-Jane.

Sarah-Ann was growing fatter; or rather, she now had some flesh on her bones. She became uncommunicative, shied away from detail, when asked about her experiences on the road. Eliza wondered what there was that she was not telling. Was her account of her flight from Ardwick the truth, the whole truth and nothing but? Something very shocking must have happened to cause Sarah-Ann to leave her husband and two daughters, of that Eliza was sure. Whether events were as she had been led to believe, she didn't quite know: those parents of William and Alfred had been kind to them all, after their flight from Birmingham. Could they have changed so much? Was there some other explanation for Sarah-Ann's desertion of her children?

But what was important was that her sister should regain health and strength and the wherewithal to feed and clothe herself. She was, Eliza acknowledged, though doing no paid work, now pulling more than her weight in the running of the household and thus relieving the rest of them of much of the burden. Eliza was enjoying her company. Sometimes it felt as if they were all girls together, as they had been back home in what seemed another lifetime.

They were, most weeks, buying a newspaper. Once read, it had many other uses: polishing windows, or shoes, insulating feet from cold or damp, stuffing into cracks, lighting fires, but the main purpose of purchase was to look for suitable positions for Sarah-Ann.

'What do you think to this one?' Sarah-Ann was by the door, using the light: the kitchen was dim, even on such a day.

She read it out, 'Wanted: a strong and active SERVANT GIRL, from the country preferred. Apply Mr Turton, 'Dog and Partridge', Liversedge Street.'

'Don't think you've got the brawny arms for shifting barrels,' Eliza said. 'Not yet, anyway.'

'This one then. "Wanted: a good PLAIN COOK, for small family, wages £14-£16. Apply Oxford Villas, Osmaston Road." '

'You could ask for an interview,' said her sister. 'Should think as a cook you'd be living in, though it doesn't say. Not that you've ever much liked cooking,' she added.

'There's a place in Sadlergate, a general registry. You know, people come and describe the sort of servant they want,' said Sarah-Ann. 'Other people who want a position tell the registry what position they'd like and the registry matches them up. It says here there's vacancies for plain cooks, housemaids, nurses and good generals.'

'Worth trying,' said Eliza. 'I think there's several of

them, registries, in Derby.'

'Now this sounds something I could do,' said Sarah-Ann after a few minutes. She read: 'Wanted, a good GENERAL SERVANT, at once, two others kept, small family, good wages. Apply 41, Burton Road.'

'At least the work'd be shared out,' said Eliza. 'You wouldn't have to do everything. Only one and you'd be worked to the bone.' She looked critically at her sister. 'We'll need to dress you up a bit, though. Black'd be best, but something better than that one.'

Sarah-Ann, though clothed respectably, was still wearing the others' cast-offs, which were not in the best of health. Eliza, since she had fled Birmingham, had worn as near to mourning clothes as she could, to give credence to her widowhood. Fortunately for her, she had already owned a black shawl, bonnet and stuff dress left from the mourning of their mother. It was considered unlucky by some to retain mourning after the mourning period ceased, a problem easily resolved for the well-off, not so for the poor, particularly the prudent poor, such as Eliza. Only since she had been spoken for by Bert, had she felt that her dress could lighten a little. Sarah-Ann, therefore, was at this moment wearing her sister's old black cotton cast-off, much mended around the cuffs, hem and elbows.

'We'll talk to Sarah when she comes in.' Sarah had gone off with her Fred Woolley for the afternoon. 'If we clubbed together, we might be able to manage something. We'll try second-hand first, a dressmaker at a pinch. Or you could make yourself something! You've all that time on your hands in the day, and somehow we'll afford the cloth.'

Sarah-Ann's face lit up. 'That's a grand idea. And it

would be new! I didn't like to ask, because of the expense, but if you're sure ... And I could pay you back when I start working. I'd like that so much.'

The click of the latch later that evening announced the arrival of Sarah. All three boys had been dispatched to bed and the three sisters were sitting out in the warm dusk of the yard, reminiscing about their childhood and going over their father and his obduracy. Sounds of merriment from the *Prince of Wales* made a cheerful backdrop. Sarah brought out a chair to join them and they told her of their plan.

Sarah pursed her lips. 'Doubt as you'd get much choice in Spondon.' she said. 'Beswicks' in Derby, now. It's in't Market Place. You could walk. Takes about an hour. Less.'

'It'd save money,' said Sarah-Ann. 'I could go any day of the week, being as I'm not working.'

'Are you strong enough yet?' inquired Diana, laying a hand on her sister's shoulder. 'We don't want you ill all over again.'

'I did all that walking to get here. Used to it now. Think as I could do, what is it? Six, eight miles all told? Might get a lift part of the way if I'm lucky. I could go to one of those registries while I'm there and see what they've got. Put my name down, maybe.'

'Well, look for Beswick's, me duck,' repeated Sarah. 'They sells all sorts o' cloth an' often remnants an' soiled stock an' such. Comes much cheaper'n you'd get elsewhere. And then there's the open Market an' the Market Hall. Friday's a market day. That'd likely work out even cheaper. But get summat as'll last'

And so it was decided. The Friday boded fair, so that Sarah-Ann set out for Derby as the other three left for the mill. They said their goodbyes as they came together through the narrow exit into Chapel Street, Sarah still repeating instructions as to the way.

Sarah-Ann waved as the others swung off towards Borrowash and Towle's Mill.

'Wouldn't mind if that was me,' said Diana, enviously. 'Just walking along, not a machine nor a bit of cotton in sight and all the shops to look into at the end of it. An' in lovely weather too.'

Their shift ended at last. At the gate they waited for each other as usual. This evening, though they would all go home for supper, Diana and Sarah would see to the boys after they'd eaten. Eliza would be called for by Bert: she too would go for a walk, a courting walk. She was looking forward to this. In fact, with every fibre of her being was she looking forward to it. She hungered now for his body. Yet, difficult though it was, she held herself back. She had lifted her skirts once and reaped disaster: she would not make that mistake again.

They wandered along through the fields, his arm round her waist, hers around his. Starlings swirled in a vast fluid shoal above their heads. Rooks flapped heavily as they settled for the night. They sat close together on a grassy bank. They became entwined in need.

'Not till we're wed,' she had to make herself say. 'You keep your hands to yourself, Bert Cope. There'll be plenty of time for that after March.'

For they had decided on the March of next year. 1884

it would be; and she wanted the time to rush towards it. Then there would come a regret as she thought of the friendship they had had between them, the three sisters and Sarah, who grew more like an older sister every day. Sarah it was who had guided them, given them the advice they had needed to make a life in this strange, quiet place.

Bert sulked for a little but she kissed him and laughed; and kissed him again and out of his sulk. He didn't hold it for long.

'Where shall we wed?' asked Eliza. She had been pondering this. 'I don't want to wed in Spondon. Too many folk who know us. I can't swear in Church that I'm a widow-woman. Because I'm not. And if I say in Spondon as I'm a spinster, they'll all know as I've been lying, an' hold it against me.'

'We could wed in Derby,' Bert said. 'No-one to know us there an' we'd 'ave a quiet wedding. Not many folk'd come; only family an' not most o' them.'

Eliza thought of her father and Emily: they'd gone all the way from Birmingham to Burton-on-Trent to marry. Had they been afraid that Emily's husband would turn up and denounce them when the vicar intoned the dreaded words, 'Speak now or forever hold thy peace'? He, the husband, Peter Ward, like Joseph Hoskinson and Sarah-Ann's William, was another who had vanished into the ether.

'I think that'd be for the best,' she said. 'I shall have Sarah for my bridesmaid. If she'd like that, of course. I wouldn't have met you if it hadn't been for Sarah.'

'An' I shall 'ave me brother William for best man. At least William can read an' write. I s'll 'ave to make a cross.

Sarah can write too. Wonder what went wrong wi' me? An' I 'ad Gaffer Douglass for a teacher, like they did. 'E used to scratch 'is 'ead o'er me. Lots o' things as I can do, but pen work's not one on 'em.'

Eliza smiled at him. 'I'll do all the pen work,' she said. 'I didn't stay on at school till I was nearly fifteen for nothing, you know. You can just make chairs an' rolling-pins an' mouse-traps an' all the other things as we'll need.'

He squeezed her hand as reply.

'We s'll try St Werburgh's,' he said. 'In Friargate.'

When Eliza was returned by Bert, she found Sarah-Ann back from her trip to the great city and holding forth.

'I've got the cloth,' she said, holding up a length of black fabric. 'It'll wear, the woman said. An' it'll wash if I have to.'

Eliza fingered the weave. It was close-knit and smooth. There's a bit of warmth there,' she said. 'And yes, I should think it'd wash. An' black's such a useful colour. Besides, you'll have to wear black as a servant. The mistress'll likely supply the apron, so as you all look alike.'

'Sarah-Ann's been telling us about that Derby balloonist,' said Diana. 'The one that shot his wife an' then himself back at the end of June.'

'I got talking to a woman in the market,' said Sarah-Ann. 'He'd had his own factory, making balloon fabric. Well-off, he was. Only the day before, he'd done a splendid ascent with his daughter. That's what they called it, 'a splendid ascent'. He was famous all over the world, travelled everywhere, Australia even. Was a professional balloonist after he'd retired from the factory. They called him the Midland Aeronaut. Came home all happy one day this last June, after he'd been up ballooning with his daughter, went to bed; an' then, after breakfast, bang an' another bang. Wife, then him. Nobody knows why.'

They shook their heads.

'An' they let the public into the house to view them in their coffins,' Sarah-Ann went on. She gave a somewhat artificial shudder before going rushing on. 'An' I had Joe's shoes mended. In the Morledge, next the coffee tavern. Soles an' heels for 6d. Left them there for a bit an' they were done when I came back.'

'Did you get the eggs?' asked Sarah.

'Six for a shilling. Bought six. Pricey, I thought. Same with butter at 1s.8d the pound. Didn't buy none of that. Oh, an' they had pheasant, 6d a brace. Have to pluck them, but it's meat an' tasty at that. Good value, I reckon. Better than rabbit - 3s.4d, two of them.'

'*And* she forgot to look at dress patterns,' said her sister, pointing an accusing finger.

'I can make the skirt alright, but the bodice might be a bit tricky.'

'I s'll ask around,' Sarah said. 'Someone'll have one as you can borrow. Or at worst you can unpick the raggy one as you're wearin' an' use that as a pattern.'

'But she remembered thread,' said Diana. 'And dress-shields, to save you under the arms.'

'Good,' they said.

'An' we've got needles,' said Sarah-Ann.

'An' what other delights can you tell of?' Eliza asked, sweetly.

'I went into this high-class shop,' said Sarah-Ann. 'The saleswomen looked at me a bit haughty-like but I didn't mind them and I went all over, just looking at things. Oh, such beautiful things.'

'Where was it?' asked Sarah.

'One of the best streets, St Peter's Street.'

'Was it Thurman and Malin?'

'That sounds right.'

'Opened about five year ago,' Sarah said. 'Only't best. It's where all't nobs go. You'll see a coachman at door waiting for 'is mistress to come out an' a footman behind all laden wi' parcels.'

'Beautiful capes,' said Sarah-Ann wistfully. 'Quilted inside, some of them. And ones made of fur, sable even. Think how that would keep you warm. And the blankets, so soft and fluffy and light; and the most beautiful colours.'

'Well,' said Eliza. 'When you've got this position and you're very rich, you can buy me a soft, furry blanket for a wedding present.'

They laughed. 'Did you find an agency?' Diana asked.

'I did, and I think as I'd be best doing what I was doing before I got married: being a servant. Housemaid, Parlour Maid, I could do that. Or General Servant. But I've no references, and the woman, she said, 'You won't get a position without references.'

'Then we'll 'ave to see as what us can do,' said Sarah. 'I s'll write you a reference; an' you,' she pointed at Eliza, 'can see to the spelling. After all, you're being a very good servant here at present. An' I s'll put 'light sewing' as one of your added accomplishments. When as you've finished that dress o' course.'

'What dost think?' Bert asked, one evening. 'Shall us

get a photograph o' young Will along on one of us? When us 'as us wedding photograph taken, I mean.'

'That would be splendid,' said Eliza. She had never had a photograph taken. It was becoming the thing to do these days though, especially when you got married and possibly for some other special occasion. They could look back on it in times to come. 'I think Will's photograph should be separate from the one of us, though.' She meant, in case people drew conclusions they were not intended to draw.

Bert assented.

Idling through the *Derby Mercury*, Eliza read a short paragraph that made her heart jump. A Spondon girl, working in the service of a Colonel Clitherow had been sent for trial at Brentford in Essex for the murder of her illegitimate child. It required no effort for Eliza to enter into the girl's desperation. That girl had not been as lucky in her friends as herself. She, Eliza, could so easily have been in her shoes. She could feel only aching pity for the girl and deep sadness at the deed. Suppose she had not kept her precious Will? Some of the thoughts she had had before his birth rose into her mind; and with shame she tried to banish them.

Village gossip revealed more details. The girl, Hannah Longdon, was the daughter of a gamekeeper working for the Drury-Lowes of Locko Park and thus a respectable man with a good position. After Hannah had left the employ of the Colonel, where she'd been a housemaid, an unpleasant smell had been noticed; and under the floorboards of a closet the body of a new-born had been discovered. Hannah had been apprehended, sent on from the Brentford court to the Central Criminal Court. Eliza waited for further news, hoping that some miracle would intervene. Late in October it came. The Grand Jury threw out the indictment for murder, keeping a lesser charge of concealing a birth. The Recorder found evidence, even for that charge, insufficient. The prisoner was discharged.

Eliza closed her eyes for thankfulness, and for the pain of it, thinking of Hannah giving birth all alone, stifling any cries for fear of discovery, panicking; and murmured a short prayer of gratitude.

It was the end of October; and the nights drawing in. It was not comfortable, indeed somewhat desolate, to be walking the lanes these days. Instead, Bert had joined them in Butts Yard, with a jug of beer bought from the *Prince of Wales*.

He also had a surprise, a bulk of something wrapped in sacking. This he spread out onto the floor, revealing dozens of tiny green hedgehogs, some splitting to reveal a smooth, brown-sheened plumpness. He was already wearing a pair of leather workman's gloves.

'If you've got a pair o' these?' he said.

They shook their heads.

'Well, I s'll do a few an' then you can take over for practice. They'll cook in't ashes under't fire.'

Joe picked up one of the 'hedgehogs' with his bare hands, feeling its sharp spines. He attempted to open it, but was defeated, reduced to sucking his prickled fingers. Bert was opening them quickly. Sarah pricked the nuts with a fork and nestled them amongst the hot ashes.

Eliza went to find mugs for the beer, then took her turn with the gloves. Even wearing those, a spine got to her now and then. Jesse cadged them from her and tried, but the gloves swamped his fingers.

'There's a tree as I knows of,' said Bert. 'They falls to't ground when they's ready.'

The scent of roasting nuts drifted alluringly from the ashes. Sarah raked one out, let it cool a little and gingerly squeezed it to test its softness. The one first ready went to Bert. They sat nibbling and savouring, making the morsels last.

'I went out today,' said Sarah-Ann. 'Testing my new dress. I was warm enough, with a shawl. I took the boys up to the schoolroom, 'cos it was the annual Sale of Work, while the children are on holiday, you know. It was interesting to see where they go every day. Jesse had some of his work on the wall, a picture. Some of the young ladies behind the stalls, they were from the vicarage, the Vicar's daughters; and there was that Mrs Cade from the Homestead; an' Mrs Cox, they said from the Hall. Proper nobs, they were. There was something called a Monster Bran Pie, where you gave thrupence and ferreted around to find a prize.'

'We just watched,' said Joe. 'A boy called Tom got some marbles, but you could buy much more'n that for thrupence.'

'There was a tree, a Christmas Tree,' put in Jesse, but they called it a Missionary Tree, and you could hang a gift on it for a missionary. We didn't though.'

'An' there was refreshments,' said Joe. 'But we didn't have none o' those, neither.' He scowled, with fierce, dark eyebrows.

'Anyway,' said Sarah-Ann, 'they raised a whole £50 for

the Bible Society, to give Bibles to foreigners that didn't have 'em, poor forsaken souls.'

'Well, that was a nice afternoon out then,' said Eliza. Joe was still scowling. She loved him when he was cross.

A case of scarlet fever came to the village; but only one, in contrast to Little Eaton, where the fever was raging. Spondon's inhabitants were reinforced in their belief that they lived in a healthy place.

Events were often held in the National Schoolroom, it being one of the few places in the village capable of accommodating a crowd. After work, one dark Saturday in late November, they all, including Bert and Fred Woolley, trooped up Chapel Street to an exhibition.

As they walked in, Will eager to see the room where the other two boys went each day, they entered a vast twittering. It amused Joe and Jesse to see cages arranged where children usually sat. The group worked their way round the exhibits, pointing out pigeons, gamecocks, poultry, canaries by the dozen, linnets, nightingales, goldfinches; which latter, Fred told them, were sure to be males, as only the males sing.

'What does they do wi' the females then?' asked Joe.

'They eats 'em,' said Fred, with relish.

In December, the Spondon and Ockbrook Choral Union chose the schoolroom as their venue for their rendering of *The Messiah* (slightly abridged). But that was on a Tuesday evening and the millworkers, their work overlapping the performance, were unable to attend.

Then it was Christmas once more. It was what was called a green Christmas, dark, dismal, wet and not very cold, the sort that was said by gloom-bearers to make for a full churchyard. There was none of the glitter and sparkle of what the elders thought of as a proper Christmas. There was no skating. Nevertheless, it had its compensations, using less fuel to try to keep warm and not having to struggle through icy drifts. This they might otherwise have had to do on Christmas Eve, that being, as it was a Monday, the one day of toil at the Mill between the finish of work on Saturday the 22nd until Thursday morning on the 27th. It did not feel just, having to break into the holiday. Still, needs must when the Devil drives, as they so often said. And, welcome as time off was, it had to be balanced by the fact that time off, unless for one of the four bank holidays, meant no pay.

It would be good to go to something festive in Derby they agreed. Could they afford it? Such delights were on offer.

There were balls a-plenty, but, as Diana pointed out, 'We'd need a Fairy Godmother and I don't think we'd have as much luck as Cinderella.'

There was the Military Band of thirty little lads, the inmates of Homes, playing selections from classics, such as Handel and Mozart, in the Drill Hall.

There was a tea with readings and recitations, to be given to 'inebriates'. But, as Diana again pointed out, they failed to qualify.

There were pantomimes: 'Whittington and his Cat' and 'Robinson Crusoe'.

However, something else caught the eye: a circus. Moreover, a circus which included a pantomime. It was on at The Circus in Prince's Street. There were to be equestrian riders, a clown with his troupe of performing dogs, followed by a pantomime to take place in the ring itself, with scenic and mechanical effects. The pantomime was called *'O'Donoghue, or The Fairy Prince of Killarney's Lake'*. It sounded magnificent, but 'All those sixpences,' said Diana, worriedly. And then it was to be held on Boxing Day and though special trains were running to take back late-night revellers, they had to think of work at seven the following morning. The boys jumped up and down and pleaded, to no effect.

However, a sop was given. They would all go into Derby on Saturday the 22nd after work and look around the shops, all of which would be decorated for the season. They would buy food and perhaps some extras for the children. They would go and return by train. At which the boys jumped up and down once more.

Accompanied by Fred and Bert they walked the holly and mistletoe streets of Derby, gazing into lighted windows overflowing with capercaillies, snipe, plover, wood-cock, black-cock, grey-hen, venison, hares, and oysters, all exhibited alongside the more usual eatables.

The windows of the Grand Clothing Hall in St Peter's Street displayed figures clad in costume from Georgian times to the present day. Grimaldi the clown sat on a huge snowball while Old Father Christmas rested, surrounded by trees and plants. In the centre of the emporium stood a huge Christmas tree.

Every step along the streets revealed another glittering display of confectionery, footwear or fancy articles.

Gradually, through the throng, they made their way to

the market where, they hoped, bargains were to be had. A goose was purchased. It would feed all, its down would be kept; and quill pens, if one had none of the modern, steel-nib kind, could be made from the flight feathers.

It would yield a vast amount of fat with multiple uses from chest-protection to cooking to the making-supple of shoe-leather - though it fell short in the rushlight department, the fat being too runny: hard mutton fat was best there. Any meat left over could be put into jars which, tops well-sealed with goose fat, would keep a while.

Oranges and nuts were found to fill the boys' stockings. Perhaps a thrupenny-bit would find its way there too.

They returned to Spondon well-satisfied, laden with parcels. The men left them to go their separate ways; the boys dragged their weary feet up from the station, up Hall Dyke, down Chapel Street, where all of a sudden, in response to some invisible sign, they stopped hanging behind, griping and moping; and spurted wildly for home.

A Victorian Miss

14
1884
SUCH BITTER-SWEET PARTINGS

Sarah-Ann found a position at last, as housemaid to a well-off Derby grocer and his wife.

'Might get to see what goes on in the shop as well,' she said. 'I've often fancied a little shop of my own.'

She set off one morning in January. Bert had taken her box – not that it contained much, but what standing would a boxless servant have? - on his shoulder down to the station the evening before, the stationmaster promising to guard it until Sarah-Ann arrived. So all she needed to carry was a second-hand bag, mended and cleaned up as best they could. It was, more fully, a carpet bag with leather handles and the wondrous ability to be unlatched at the sides and used as a rug.

'In case your new Mistress is an old miser,' said Diana, in her usual cheerful way.

Sarah-Ann, having arrived on their doorstep with

nothing, had few possessions. She would not be the only servant: there were several others. There would thus be some companionship, she hoped. As a lone servant in a household, working all hours, life could be very bleak: you could hardly gossip with the mistress and there was almost no time to meet anyone else.

Eliza did not envy her sister. Mill work might involve long hours of wearying tedium, but at least when it finished, it *was* finished, until the next specific starting time; and the space between, however short, was your own. There were plenty of people to get to know and to talk with as you went to and fro. She wondered whether she would miss it when she was married. Bert did not want her to continue at the mill. He was the breadwinner, he said. He would provide: it was demeaning for a wife to have to earn money towards the household.

He already had his eye on a house. It was in Moor Street, No.8, a five-roomed house, superior to this one, although it would be housing far fewer people. They would be leaving Bert's younger brother Charlie behind in Butts Yard; though they would be gaining in Cope terms, as at No.7 Moor Street lived another Charlie, a cousin of some sort, with wife and four children. And at No.9 lived another cousin, John, with wife and two children. Both men worked on the railway.

Eliza was still slightly hazy as to the spider-web of Cope relationships. Should she and Bert ever have children, one of them would no doubt be a Charlie: it was a Cope name, sanctified by tradition. Herbert was an obvious choice. William, another Cope name, she had already gifted to her first son. John, then; or perhaps a

Henry, always known as Harry, more usually 'Arry. She liked Harry. Why did people give their children names beginning with an aitch, while knowing they'd never use it? 'Oraces and 'Enrys, 'Arriets and 'Annahs abounded.

And, she thought, if asked what letter began the name Harry, 'Arrys would most likely say, 'Haitch,' making an explosively laboured use of that first letter. Those accustomed to calling a Harry 'Harry' would say, controversially, 'aitch,'. It was all rather odd.

Diana seemed restless after Sarah-Ann left. 'I don't know what I'll do when you and Bert are married,' she said suddenly one day.

It was a Sunday; and they had finished their dinner after returning from Chapel. Joe and Jesse had set off on some mysterious mission of their own; and Bert was coming to collect his intended before they went for a cup of tea and a gossip at the house of some or other member of the clan.

'I'm thinking of writing to Father,' she said. 'I've a wanting to see him again. I know he was bad to you, but I'm still fond of him for all that.'

Eliza, taken aback, said nothing, and waited; and she went on, 'In fact I've already written to him. I can't live with you an' Bert. Not right at the start anyway, I can't. You don't want your sister there at all hours. You don't. You need time to yourselves.'

'I don't know what to say.' It had been assumed, without being spoken of, that Diana would live with herself and Bert.

'I might come back, you know, if things don't go well. I'll get work down there, but I could live with them, Father and her. See how it goes, anyway. And the Mill won't seem the same without you and Sarah. I should feel left behind somehow. Lonely. I'd rather start again somewhere else.'

'I shall miss you so much,' said Eliza, the import of this news beginning to tell. 'You've been the best sister in the world to me.'

She felt tearful. Why did things have to change so? Yes, she wanted to marry Bert, but that decision had changed a whole way of life in which six people, seven if you counted Sarah-Ann, had been mostly happy. Still, a small something whispered that she would like best to be on her own with just Bert and Will, for a while at least.

There's one thing *I'll* not miss,' said Diana. Eliza looked at her inquiringly. 'Fluff!' said Diana triumphantly. 'I can give up all and every single bit of cotton fluff to the end of my days.'

'You can always come back,' Eliza said bravely. 'If things don't work out, you know. But I hope they will. Tell him I'm getting married, won't you?'

Then a thought struck her. 'But you are coming to the wedding, aren't you? Oh, you must do that.'

'I've thought,' said Diana. 'And the best thing is, I think, to see you an' Bert get wed an' then leave for Birmingham after. Till then I can help.'

What should she wear on this coming important day in her life? Ladies nowadays tended to emulate the Queen, who had married in 1840 in white satin and Honiton lace, orange-blossom and diamonds, but they were ladies and could afford such things, or pale imitations. Those such as Eliza must be more prudent. Besides, to marry in white would be mockery. She determined to have a new gown at least. But what colour? She consulted the cognoscenti.

Diana positioned herself at a distance and scrutinised her sister. 'I think,' she said at last, 'that you look well in dark blue. Or a rich, glowing sort of brown, chestnut, to go with your hair. Just like our mother's, your hair is. Green would look pretty, but it's unlucky, so not that, not for a wedding. There's troubles enough without inviting them. Not that I think you'll have any,' she added, 'with Bert being Bert; but you can't be too careful.'

Sarah nodded her head at each point made. 'Go an' see what there is in't way o' materials,' she said. 'Either blue or brown, I'd say. Dost want woollen or summat more dressy, to keep for best, like?'

Diana clapped her hands. 'Oh, Liza, you could get a heavy grosgrain. It needn't have a train, just a bustle of course, really plain. You could dress it up with lace cuffs and lace at the neck for the wedding. It'd wear for years. Oh, do. Do have something pretty for once. We could all help to buy the material an' we could all work on it. Or you could get a proper dressmaker to make it, just this one time. We must make you look lovely on your wedding day, mustn't we, Sarah?'

There was also the photograph to consider. The dress must look good on the photograph, considering that it would be there to be looked at for many, many years.

'Will needs something new too,' said Eliza, 'Bert says he's to have his photograph taken as well.'

Discussion decided on velvet for Will, a frock of a colour to complement that of his mother, tied in at the waist, with lace trim around the neck and sleeves. Pantaloons of matching velvet would be worn below the dress. His boots would have to do, well-polished.

And the dressmaker? Who should she be? It was a foregone conclusion. A family member should be entrusted with the honour. She would benefit from the money: Eliza would benefit from care taken and a fair price.

'Mary 'Oskison,' said Sarah flatly. 'Lives up Brandy Lane off Church Street, where me dad lives. Calls 'erself 'Oskison 'stead of 'Oskinson, but she was married to my Joseph's son by 'is first wife. Widow now for definite. 'Er Robert died, oh, six, seven year ago when 'e were only twenty-five. That I do know. Married not even three year they were. Two little boys to feed.'

'Is there anybody in Spondon you aren't kin to?' asked Diana. 'An' anybody as you don't know nothing about?'

'Not a lot, one way an' t'other,' said Sarah, with a grimace of acknowledgement.

Sarah accompanied Eliza to Brandy Lane a few evenings later. Mary Hoskison opened the door to their knock and beckoned them in. The tiny parlour was strewn with garments-in-the-making. There was one still held under the needle of a treadle sewing machine. A gas-lamp hissed brightly above.

She was a slight, neat woman, smiled as Sarah introduced them. 'Been my trade for many a year,' she said. 'Gave it up when I married my Robert, but 'ad to take to it again when 'e died. An' what I'd a done without it, the Good Lord only knows. Now, what can I do for you?'

The mission was explained, women's magazines were leafed through for styles, fabrics were shown, their qualities discussed. Decisions were made. Eliza was measured. The dressmaker would obtain the cloth: she had contacts. A price was agreed. Eliza would come again for a fitting. She would bring Will with her to be measured too: the price to be charged was very reasonable.

They left, hearing the sound of the treadle start up and grow fainter as they walked along the street.

'I s'll be leaving come the end of February,' Sarah announced. 'Fred an' me, we've found a place in St Werburgh's Churchyard, St Werburgh's in Derby, that is. We thought as you could use it for your address when the banns come to be called. 'Cause you'll need one, you know, an address. An' you can stay there the night before the wedding. You an' Will.'

'You are so good to me, Sarah. What my life would have come to without you, well, I dread to think. I do so hope we'll always be friends. I wish you joy of Fred: he's a lucky man.'

'An' 'e'll take the lads. Like Bert's takin' Will. Better'n some men, they are, both on 'em.'

They walked on, up Hall Dyke, following their thoughts.

'St Werburgh's is where I married my Joseph,' said Sarah, ruminatively. 'I 'ope as you 'as better luck wi' me brother.'

Eliza linked an arm into that of her friend. They walked on.

'Tell you what,' said Sarah suddenly. 'You'll keep anything as is yours now, after you marry Bert. An 'usband's got no right to everything as you own, not like it used to be. Was like that when I married my Joseph only ten year ago. Not that 'e sold me silver 'airbrushes an' me diamonds to keep 'im in beer; but 'e could a done. If I'd 'ad any, an' if 'e'd 'ad a mind. One bad thing, though. If you gets into debt, you'll 'ave to pay it back yersen, 'stead of 'im, as it used to be. Only come into law a year back.'

'Times do change,' Eliza said. 'Mostly for the better. What do you think?'

"Ospitals is better. Give you summat now afore they cuts a leg off. Give you summat when you're 'avin' a baby, thanks be to the good Queen - if they think as you really needs it, an' if they feels like givin' it, an' if it's 'andy, o' course.'

'An' all that pain's on account of that Eve and her listening to that snake. All us women have to suffer for ever and ever, so they tells us, just 'cause *she* made that one mistake. An' I'm certain sure I never even laid eyes on the woman.'

The dress progressed. Will was taken to the lady with the long tape, who wrapped it round his chest, neck and waist in turn and stood him on a chair to measure him from top to bottom, scribbling with a stub of pencil the while.

'The blue will suit him,' the lady said. 'Him being so fair.'

They had decided on a deep, rich blue for both of them. Will would be at the ceremony, though in the company of Fred, along with Sarah's boys, Sarah being a witness with more important things to do. The Curate would never realise that he belonged to the bride.

Sarah left for Derby, and her new life with Fred, at the end of a week. They hugged, she and Eliza and Diana. The house in Butts Yard felt empty without her and Joe and Jesse. Eliza was glad she would be moving: this house would be full of ghosts.

Time off was money lost and so they had decided on a Sunday, the second of March, as the wedding day. That left the Saturday afternoon for them to get over to Derby, for photographs to be taken; and meant that more people would be able to attend, should they so wish. They could be back in Spondon, in their new home, by the Sunday evening, when all who would might come a-calling. Bert would be able to be back at work on the Monday morning, whilst she would be a lady of leisure. The new house even boasted an outside wash-house of its very own with a fire-space under a copper boiler.

It had not escaped Eliza's notice that this was a Leap Year. The last Leap Year had been 1880, when, in its own month of March, she had made a near-fatal mistake. But she was so much older now ... and then thought that she wasn't that much older at all, only honed a little towards wisdom. She was twenty-seven, Bert twenty-nine. She prayed that on this journey into uncharted waters they would both prove wise enough.

On the Friday night before the wedding, she bathed Will in the tub before the kitchen range, washed his hair and then sat him on a stool with a towel draped around him while Diana, the one considered to have flair, carefully cut his hair. It was straight and fine so that she had to be careful with the scissors.

'How's that?' she said at last, standing away from her now-fidgeting subject. Eliza murmured her appreciation.

'Can I go now?' whined the model. And departed, without procrastination, to bed.

Saturday dawned: the last day at the Mill. The day was mild and the sun beginning to warm the earth; farm workers were planting potatoes.

A whip-round had been made; and at lunchtime, as they finished their work, Eliza was presented with a small sewn bag exuding a clink of coins. All gathered round, wishing her well and Eliza tried to thank them, but turned away in tears.

'Eh, me duck, it's never that bad!' someone shouted; and Eliza smiled through her tears.

'I shall miss you all,' she said. 'You've been such kind friends.'

'Well, I'm not goin' nowhere,' said one voice. 'An' don't you go bein' so 'oity-toity as you can't speak to us now you're a married woman.'

There was a laugh. They started off home in good spirits, laughing, jostling, quips rending the air.

A bag had already been packed with overnight things for Will and herself, with Will's velvet and the precious dress shrouded in tissue paper. Eliza, Will and Diana left the house and walked up Chapel Street to the top of Hall Dyke where Bert awaited them, having walked from his lodgings in Stanley Highway.

As they drew nearer, Eliza noticed a slight difference in her betrothed. His ears had become much less visible in the past weeks, but the shaggy hair which had been growing over them had been trimmed; and not to its normal small-basin-cut.'

'Well, aren't you the handsome bridegroom? Been to a proper barber, I see. And about time too,' said Diana, impudently.

'Saucy baggage,' returned her brother-in-law-to-be. But his mouth twitched.

Down the Dyke they went, happy in the dry, bright air, into Potter Street, then turning left towards the station where they would meet Bert's best man, his older brother William: it wasn't far.

'Next time you walk this way you'll be a married woman,' said Bert, and squeezed her arm protectively.

'An' I wonder what that'll be like?' taunted Eliza.

Bert laughed, swung her round and kissed her. 'Bit like that,' he said. 'But better.'

In Derby the party made for Sarah and Fred's cottage in St Werburgh's Churchyard: Bert and his brother would head for their own separate lodgings, round the corner in Ford Street, later on. In the cottage that overlooked the Church they would enter tomorrow, Eliza, Bert and little William each re-dressed in their wedding finery. Having been much admired, and admired in particular by the ladies of the party, they next ventured into the town, their object the grand premises of '*Mr Will.m En.d Swift, Artiste Photographer, Miniature and Portrait Painter. Of Skegness and 30, St. Peter's Street, Derby*'. It was not hard to find.

They went through the portal with a sense of awe, were bowed to and bidden 'Come this way, Sir, Madam', almost as if they were gentry. Bert and Eliza had their likenesses taken first, she sitting, he standing, his hand resting on her shoulder.

Then it was Will's turn. He was positioned beside something that looked like the arm of a very grand sofa with the rest of it unaccountably missing. He was given the swag to grasp and told to stand very still and not to smile: he was far too awed and overcome by the importance of the occasion to do any other. Then there was a flash. A three-year-old Will-in-velvet was captured for eternity.

He looked at his mother, appealing. He was told he could move, at which he wailed, 'Don't like it,' and ran to bury his face in his mother's skirts.

The photographs would be posted to their new home.

The frock-coated photographer bowed them out, wishing them all health and happiness in their new life.

'An' what shall us do now?' asked Bert, as they walked, her arm in his, Will's hand clutching hers, into the bustling street.

15
1947
THE FURTHEST SHORE

She would be late for the mill! She reached out an anxious arm for Diana. But the rest of the bed was empty. As the upstairs front of 26 Waugh Street, Ancoats, dissolved, so the present slowly resolved itself to take its place. She opened her eyes for a moment to ascertain reality; and gratefully and luxuriously closed them again.

The bed in the upstairs back room of the rectory wrapped her in its comfort. She drowsed. Morning sun chinked through the heavy curtains. An eiderdown had slipped half off. With an effort, she put out a hand to tug it back, noticing with distaste the bones visible through the transparent skin, the dark blotches they called grave spots.

She had no need to get up, would doze until Harry arrived with her morning tea. He was a good son, Harry.

She snuggled anew into the warmth and slipped back into the dreaming.

From nowhere appeared sister Sarah-Ann on her wedding day, blooming with youth and expectation. The image faded into that of a much older Sarah-Ann in the little grocer's shop that she ran for years in Derby.

Why had Sarah-Ann left those daughters behind in Manchester? Had she told her sisters the truth of it? Thank goodness the little girls had been looked after; by the grandparents up there to start with. Then Alfred, their uncle, who was Will's father, had taken the older one, after he'd married. That was generous, of him and his wife both.

The younger had been taken in by the other grandfather, old John Kirby in Aston. That was a surprise. No-one would have thought he'd show tenderness to a girl. Though this one had been conceived in wedlock and maybe that softened his heart.

Poor man, she thought suddenly*: he must have been so disappointed in Sarah-Ann and me. Not one daughter gone to the bad, but two! He put so much store in being respectable. And how sad for him that he'd had no sons to help in the business, raise the family in the world.* She was glad that he'd prospered in his latter years, with his second family: builder and contractor.

As for the motives for looking after Sarah-Ann's daughters - Alfred might have been prompted, in part at least, by his conscience, taken the one little girl in as a good deed in recompense for a bad; that of leaving herself in the lurch, pregnant and unmarried.

A Victorian Miss

And John Kirby, who had taken the other, surely had something on *his* conscience to compensate for: casting her out. Even if she had failed him, throwing her into the street had been extreme. Had that shawl, flung after her onto the cobbles, been a gesture of contempt, as she'd always thought? Or had it been to help protect her? A spark of love? And was that pound, that he'd once sent for Will, a peace-offering? She'd never know now: both Alfred and her father were long gone. And … sleeping dogs. She'd often wondered, though.

Alfred had joined the police force, as he'd wanted. He'd soon become a sergeant. He must have matured, with the responsibilities of the job and of marriage and children. Still, after all these years, she could remember the shape and feel of his body, the texture of that rough coat he wore. And his voice: 'Cariad, oh cariad.' And his humour. She'd thought him much older than seventeen

Oh, well, that too was so long ago. Alfred had been thrown from a bicycle, she'd heard, and died of it, way back in the second year of the Great War. When men were dying daily by the thousand out there in the mud, he'd fallen from a bicycle in the safety of Blighty. He'd retired from the Manchester City Police Force by then and was pursuing the blameless occupation of School Attendance Officer. A pint or two in a pub after work, cycling dutifully home to his wife; and the Angel of Death lying in wait.

She'd told Will that Alfred George was his real father, when she judged he was old enough to understand: he had a right to know. His father, she'd said, was the reason for his middle name, Alfred. And Will had always kept to the Kirby, the surname he'd had when they first came to Spondon, when she'd given out that she was a widow.

Bert had been a good substitute father to him. Stepfathers could be cruel, hating the chick already in the nest, something primitive she supposed. But Bert was never cruel. And Will had turned out alright. Even though he'd been born the wrong side of the blanket, it didn't seem to have ever counted against him. Some children, it ruined their lives.

She could picture him as he'd be at this very moment: smart, as he always liked to be, in shirt, tie and waistcoat beneath the protection of a stout, buff cotton coat with plenty of pockets. There he stands, in her mind, hands apart as he leans forward over the counter of his general store in Chapel Street; he and a customer, chuckling together.

Will'd never moved more than a few steps from Chapel Street. Except for being dragged off unwillingly to France, of course. And he was doing well, had that big house and garden behind the shop, both made beautiful by his pretty wife who had a passion for flowers and liked good things.

Will was respected in the village; and they all loved his mimicry of village characters in the shows they put on in the Village Hall. Rolled in the aisles, they did. Did he inherit that aspect of himself from Alfred? Or was a whisper of it from her own long-gone mother, who had been able to drive John Kirby out of his dark moods by teasing him, coaxing him, into a reluctant smile?

She smiled now to herself as she remembered Will's quandary: whom should he give as his father on his approaching marriage certificate? It would never do to mortally offend his future father-in-law, respected, God-fearing, non-smoking, teetotal elder of his Chapel. Between them they'd decided on George Kirby as the name of his father. It was something of a truth. And no-one noticed the discrepancy between that and the John Kirby she'd given him for a parent on his birth certificate.

Eliza's thoughts skipped back again to Sarah-Ann. The fates seemed to have stranded her in a backwater. She'd met a chap after she'd gone to Derby, lived with him for years, she running the grocer's shop – she'd always fancied a shop, Sarah-Ann.

They never had any children; and the husband had died only a few months after they'd finally made themselves legal. She carried on with the shop for another twelve years. Died just before the last War. Seventy-seven. What a dull time of it she'd had. Still, maybe it had suited Sarah-Ann.

Eliza drowsed. It was good to drowse; and it was not very reprehensible at her time of life: the year had turned to 1947 last month and she would be ninety-one come September.

The upstairs front in Ancoats came back into her head again in as much detail as if she'd left it yesterday; fireless and cold as doom in the winter, cramped and scantily furnished, washing hung across the room to dry, so that you ducked under its heavy wetness going from door to window.

Harry, here at the rectory, had someone in to do all that, washing and such. And he was always called Harry,

Janet Goldfinch

not 'Arry, as she'd feared he would be; certainly not now when he was a respected clergyman.

There were a lot more rooms here than they'd had in Ancoats. Or anywhere else she'd lived, come to that. Not that this was a wealthy living: the inhabitants of Seagrave numbered less than three hundred and fifty. It was, though, modestly comfortable and, Harry being a bachelor, he didn't have to spend money on more than the two of them.

She could still do a little round the house, a little cooking here and there, a little sewing and mending, tidying; and she'd never wanted much in the way of material things. Which was just as well, she told herself, because if she *had*, she would have been a very disappointed old woman.

Suppose Harry had been living in the old rectory, the house they now called Seagrave Hall that backed onto the churchyard? Lovely house it was. They would have rattled around in that like two peas in a barrel, she and Harry, much worse than here. A daily help wouldn't have been much use in that place. Never have coped. A vicar who lived there once, named Burton, had written a famous book. What was it called? Something less than cheerful. Yes, *The Anatomy of Melancholy*. Harry had a copy. She'd opened the book but had given up after the first few sentences.

There'd been someone famous who'd lived in Ancoats. When it was at its worst, just before her time there. He'd been horrified by the poverty he saw. He'd written a book about poverty. And he'd helped to invent communism, which, like socialism, was supposed to make working people's lives better; although it didn't seem to have done that in Russia by all accounts, and most people were afraid of it. What was his name?

Seagrave, she thought, was a little like Spondon, though smaller. Had the Rev. Burton been driven to melancholy because he lived here?

Harry didn't appear to suffer from melancholy: rather the opposite. He now, he had turned out as a surprise.

There'd been Will, of course, her first child, who was Alfred's son, and then, after she married Bert, there'd been Charlie, who now worked for the railway, then Harry.

Memory of the two dead baby sons still pulled at her heart. And there was the sadness of Emily, her last child, who'd not quite made the year. She'd have liked a daughter to talk to. Odd, how her father's most despised daughter had been the one to give birth to five boys.

Both Will and Charlie were ordinary working men. But Harry, her third son, was something different. And he had cemented her respectability. No-one, knowing of her as the Rector's Mother, could ever have viewed her as less than respectable. True, there might have been murmurs that total abstinence from alcohol might better become a Rector's Mother. But surely, when one had survived so much, one could afford a slight lapse from virtue now and again?

She snuggled anew into the warmth, hoping to resume fair dreams; and slipped back once more into the past. The past seemed to occupy her more and more these days

Diana now, the youngest of the three of them, the bright and sunny one, she'd been the first of them to quit

229

this world. To think of Diana stirred a great weight of half-buried guilt: she should never have let Diana leave Spondon. She'd gone back down South to live with their father, the one daughter who hadn't failed him.

The wave of fate had tossed Diana up at first: she'd married a baker and life seemed set fair. But then the baker had died, even before their one child had reached his third birthday. It was a boy, though John Kirby hadn't lived long enough to see him. How the fates played tricks!

Diana, sweet, blameless Diana and the boy, had struggled on, becoming poorer and poorer, ending up in a tiny, three-roomed house in a slum court in Birmingham. Diana had never owned the piano she had dreamed of. Instead, she had sunk into the dregs of life, clinging to existence by charring and taking in lodgers. Imagine, living-kitchen and two bedrooms, with two of you and a couple of lodgers. She could hardly bear to think of it: it was Ancoats all over again. It was back to despair and clawing mere survival from a grim and unforgiving place. True, there were fates even worse than Diana's, but she had fallen very low. And she, her sister, had not come to the rescue. Alfred and her father were not alone in having things to regret.

All three sisters had got out of Ancoats, but fate had borne her, Eliza, on an upward wave. Diana had been sucked under. Her boy had died in the spring of 1914, some disease or other sweeping the slums clean of their miserable human occupants; and his mother had quickly followed him. The boy was sixteen. Well, the best you could say was that he was spared the Western Front, she supposed. Imagine, not having known about the first of the Wars, never mind the second.

A Victorian Miss

She'd loved Diana, always cheerful and willing, such an optimistic outlook on life she'd had. She'd been so helpful in those years when she, Eliza, had struggled with the effects of that one false step with Will's father. Why was it that she had had a far more comfortable life than her sisters?

When you thought about it, that one March evening in 1880 had changed the course of all their lives. She remembered the old warning: 'For want of a nail', leading to the loss of a kingdom: large consequences could be triggered by small events. If she had not become a fallen woman that March evening, what might life have been like, for all the sisters? She slipped away into sleep.

Eliza woke again. She stretched a little. A cup of tea sat cooling on the bedside table. The eiderdown had to be hauled back. Why did they cover eiderdowns in satin? They looked lovely, but caused a lot of slippery annoyance.

Harry must have been and gone. Had he really had a letter from Our Gracie yesterday? Or had that been a dream? It had the unlikeliness of one.

Someone had pulled back the curtains and she saw, through the window of the bedroom, that the sky had greyed heavily over. She gazed at the tree branches, each black bone almost invisible through its shroud of snow. Surely spring and the green of their budding could not be not far off? Though even as the longing came to mind, a few fresh flakes began to fall.

Gracie was not a dream, though as improbable as one. What wild caprice of the fates had put her in Harry's path? How was it that her Harry knew someone so famous?

How was it that a country vicar, with a penchant for plus-fours and for the embroidering of tablecloths, had caught, and kept over years, the attention of a woman of world renown?

Had they met during the Great War? All her boys, Will, Charlie and Harry, had been through that hell. And all of them had returned. It was a miracle, when you thought how many had not come back. Even the Drury-Lowes, the grand folk at Spondon's Locko Hall, had lost a son. Who was she, to have kept her three beloved boys, while the gentry suffered? Sister Diana and her son, she reminded herself, had not lived to see the start of even the Great War. How strange, she thought again, not to have known there was to be one. Not for certain.

Harry had been through the Great War but not the next: he had been vicar-ing then, not fighting. And he'd have been too old to go, as had been his brothers, thank the Lord. Gracie, of course, had not sung for the troops in the Great War, so she couldn't have met Harry there.

Gracie Fields was so famous: on the stage, in variety, in films. She'd sung all through the Second World War, songs about Sally and aspidistras, waving people goodbye, baking cakes and the twelfth of never, rather haunting, that one. Eliza began to hum in her creaky voice and changed to the Isle of Capri. Harry had been to the Isle of Capri, to stay at Gracie's villa. She had come to Seagrave and opened bazaars or fêtes for him.

Of course! She remembered now. Gracie Fields had been playing in Leicester and Harry had asked her to judge his annual children's fancy-dress parade. When he was curate of St. Chad's in the town, he'd always managed to inveigle pantomime leads to act as judges.

One year it was Dan Leno, who'd come in costume as Widow Twankey.

And when Harry moved from St. Chad's to Seagrave, he'd carried on asking famous people, like Gracie or, in want of stars, Lady this or the Duchess of that to open the bazaar or fête.

Those fêtes! Harry always had a raffle, the prize hopefully provided by someone of fame and fortune. He embroidered rather lovely tablecloths; and every year one would feature as a prize or on a stall. Or it might be an embroidered cushion-cover, or a tea-cosy in raffia, in the guise of a thatched cottage drowning in roses, hollyhock and lupin. Every household in the village must have owned at least one of them. A stifled giggle escaped her at a vision of a village visitor entering another cottage, knowing full well that she would be served tea from a pot kept warm by a flower-draped, raffia cottage, just like her own, upon an embroidered tablecloth, the twin of hers. She shouldn't be so disrespectful: he meant well, did her boy Harry.

He'd got All Saints out of debt with his celebrities, as he'd done St. Chad's.

And how was it that Harry had become attracted to religion in the first place? Even as a child, he'd been a keen member of his Bible class. True, she and Bert had been chapel-goers for a while and on special occasions, at least while the boys were young. But neither she nor Bert had been what you might call devout. Chapel, or Church, was just something you did, so as not to be unusual. It was a place where you could sit in a pew dressed in your best while closing your eyes for a surreptitious morning snooze, and feel no guilt at being without employment. It was a place where you met people and had days out in the summer: she remembered those horse-drawn omnibuses before the Great War, laden with folk dressed in their best, trundling a few miles to a field and a picnic and everyone singing, especially on the return journey.

They'd taken most of the country's horses for that first war, commandeered them. Will's own precious horses had been taken: he'd kept the brasses to remember them by. They hung each side of the fireplace in his dining room and were kept polished by his wife. On festival days he'd plaited the horses' manes and tails and brushed their coats till they glistened. They'd looked a treat. He'd had a trap and took Minnie and the girls out into the country, the horse smartly trotting. They had all worn hats. Everyone did of course, but Minnie's were special, her coming from a hatting family.

When Will left school, he'd started in firewood. She smiled, remembering how, in the old Butts Yard days, it had been the boys' task to fetch kindling. She remembered too the cart that Bert had made for Will: it had something to answer for, that cart. Will had needed a proper, large cart for his firewood, and for the coal he'd graduated to. He'd rented a field nearby to keep his horses, and in summer when the grass grew long, he'd scythed it down and he and Minnie and the girls had gone a-haymaking. They'd loved that, those girls, her granddaughters.

When Will had come back from the Western Front - and there the fates had tossed her beloved son to within a hair's breadth of death, for they nearly shot him as a deserter, only they changed their minds. Because of course he was no deserter: his convoy had been ambushed and Will had managed to make his way back to his regiment on foot. It just took him a long time, with being in a strange country and not knowing where he was. Ten days, he said.

What peculiar lives people did have. You'd never predict them, lives never ran straight on the rails, so to speak.

Anyway, when Will got back from the Western Front, he'd worked at the Colour Works, worked for a boss for the only time in his life. In her mind she saw again the small boy, determined to splash in puddles, in the stream. He'd never been happy at being told what to do.

He'd saved up enough money at the Colour Works to start out on his own again. Market trader first, then a little shop, then a bigger one. And he now had a van. He'd learnt to drive before the Great War, besides having the horses, which was why he'd been in that convoy of lorries carrying supplies when it had been ambushed. His mate had jumped out one side and was shot. He'd jumped out the other and run. And got lost. And there she was again with Will being threatened with a firing squad, and what might have been. It didn't bear thinking about.

Where was she? She'd been puzzling about Harry becoming religious. Yes, he'd come back from the War, returned to the Colour Works for about three years while it grew in his head that he wanted to be a clergyman. He'd trained, or whatever you call it, at the Theological College at Lichfield. They were so proud, she and Bert - at least Bert had lived to see that - when, in 1922 Harry was ordained a priest. She saw the day, all solemn and grand, the music and the rolling words, the majesty of the cathedral. A clergyman, and in the Church of England too! Mixing with the gentry, who'd have thought it?

Such a lovely church was Harry's. All Saints. Very small, very old. They'd found a stone altar half-buried in the churchyard. From Anglo-Saxon times, it was, turned out at a time when ideas of religion had changed. A thousand years of babies had been christened in the font! And there were two strange musical instruments in a glass case, from the time before churches had organs. A serpent, one was called.

And here she now was, beached at last, you might say; living in luxury, a person of dignity, of respect. Harry wasn't ashamed of his old mother, even though she'd once been what they called these days 'an unmarried mother' and moreover cast out by her only living parent. Not that that was blazoned abroad, naturally. Still, it was odd where the wave cast you up. And why you? Why not the equally worthy Sarah-Ann, or Diana?

Eliza slipped again into sleep and when she woke noticed the plate on the bedside table. Had she drunk that tea earlier? She could not remember. She raised herself with some difficulty. How annoying it was to grow old. Why did one's muscles have to weaken, along with sight and hearing? And mind, she supposed, though she hadn't noticed that particularly herself. Though she wouldn't, she thought on reflection. It was for others to notice that.

The plate held sandwiches. Goodness, was that the time? She consulted the clock with the large dial that stood behind the plate. Half past one. Good gracious: she must get up. What was she doing lying abed like this?

In the days at the mill, that would never have done. She might have lost her job. She would have had her wages docked at the least. That would have spelt disaster. She had had to work, for Will and for herself. Even if you felt under the weather you had to force yourself to work. No matter how tired you felt, or how old you were, you had to work. Things were different now: there was that thing of joy and gratitude, an Old Age Pension.

Though people had had to put in long hours during the War, she reminded herself, and still were doing, even though it had been over for a good year. Not much was yet off ration. Some people thought life was as hard as it had been while the War was on, even though it was officially Peace Time. The bombings had stopped, thank goodness, though Spondon hadn't seen much of that. Derby had though, with the Germans trying to bomb Rolls Royce that made the aircraft engines; and with Spondon only three miles away they had heard and seen enough.

When she woke up again, the plate was still sitting there, holding its sandwiches. She was not hungry.

Where was Harry? Quite likely, she re-assured herself, Harry had cycled to the station en route to Loughborough, where he'd often go to fetch a bit of fish for Mrs So-and-So or a ball of wool for Mrs Somebody-Else. She hoped he would bring back a bottle or two of stout: she liked a glass of stout of an evening. Strengthening, they said it was. She pictured him cycling powerfully along in those plus-fours he was so fond of. They suited him, she thought; dashing was the word, although they were becoming less fashionable nowadays. It was a pity he'd never married: he would have made somebody an excellent husband. But then, she reflected, wives did not always get on with their mothers-in-law and she might not have had the position she held now. Maybe things were for the best.

She felt warm even though it was winter. It was a very solid house and held the heat and she had plenty of bedclothes: sheets and blankets and that shiny eiderdown. Besides, she had on a warm viyella nightdress, a bed-jacket and bed-socks knitted by herself, the latter reconstituted from one of Harry's old pullovers: she still had the habit of turning one thing into another as long as there was a spark of life in it. She also had the luxury of one of those earthenware hot-water bottles to get into bed with, though it was cold now and she had pushed it down beyond her feet. She stretched. It might have fallen out: she couldn't find it. Good bedclothes were a blessing. Not enough thanks were given to them.

It had been very cold, even for December. And now it was the end of January and even colder. She did not remember cold of such ferocity since the boys were young, early 1895 it would have been. There had been a deal of skating and tobogganing then!

She felt the cold these days, especially since everyone was having to be so careful with coal. Electricity, which had come to Seagrave only just prior to the last War, had recently been cut off for part of the day. The radio wasn't broadcasting all day either. It was the snow, the great drifts piling up so that coal couldn't get from the mines to the power stations or out to the people.

She gave up the idea of Harry cycling along the roads:

he wouldn't be able to. Which meant there would be no stout, unless Harry bought it from the *White Horse* next to the Church. Then the fact would be all round the village in half an hour. There were disadvantages in being a vicar's mother.

Her mind reverted to the cottage in Butts Yard: that had been a cold place in winter with its flimsy walls and ill-fitting windows. They'd made rag rugs to keep the cold at bay, the cold that kept coming up through the floors. They had been good times those, nevertheless: the three of them and the children, organising their own lives, sharing. It was one of the periods in her life she would not have minded re-living.

And she and Bert had gone back to live on that very spot, near as made no difference, after the Yard'd been pulled down and made into Gladstone Road. No.1 they'd lived at.

There was something warm by her side. She felt it. It was another of those Denby stoneware hot-water bottles, snug in its towelling suit which prevented you burning yourself. She didn't remember it being put there, but there it was. There was another at her feet, she realised. Someone had closed the curtains, cutting her off from the outside and there was a tiny glimmer flickering on the ceiling: there must be a fire in the small iron grate. Never before had there been such a thing; and the coal in such short supply!

Sarah had found the coal for them, that first week they had spent in Spondon. Sarah had been almost like a mother to her and Diana. If it hadn't been for Sarah, where would she be now?

Sarah Hoskinson she had been then, when Eliza knew her in Manchester, Sarah Cope she'd been born as. If she, Eliza, hadn't known Sarah in Manchester and if they hadn't come back to Sarah's home village, she would never have met Bert Cope, who was Sarah's brother. And then she wouldn't have had Charlie and Harry and spent just a few days short of forty-five years with her Bert; and she certainly wouldn't have been living in this rectory.

Somehow the wave, after dashing her on the harsh rock of 'scarlet woman', had picked her up and tossed her alongside Sarah for a while; until the wave had parted them again, she to marry Bert, and Sarah to go to Derby to live with Fred Woolley. They never did marry, Fred's wife being still alive and living in Spondon; though they'd had two sons to add to Sarah's Joe and Jesse. It seemed that not everyone was living the life of 'till death do us part' and 'in holy wedlock', as you were supposed to do, though they all pretended to of course and woe betide you if the tongues began wagging.

Fred was another who departed this life before his time; and two years later Sarah lost her eldest boy, Joe. Eliza felt a twinge of sadness: she'd been fond of Joe and his dark scowl. Only seventeen he was: what a waste. Jesse, the younger, had married and had children; though she, Eliza, had outlived him, too.

Sarah never went out to work again after she'd left the mill: loved and cared-for, her maternal nature always to the fore, she ran the household whilst Fred or her children brought the money in. She'd reached seventy-three, not too bad an age.

But she, Eliza, had been the lucky one. Of all those she knew when she had arrived in Ancoats, she was the only one left alive. All were gone.

Perhaps when the earth had shaken off its snow and the endless, lazy days of sun had returned to grace outdoor gatherings such as Church fêtes, she, Eliza, might meet Our Gracie in person. Would the wave bear her on its crest that far? Life was so bizarre, who could tell?

How was it that she, Eliza, had seen ninety years pass? Who could have foretold her prodigious transformation from Fallen Woman into Rector's Mother?

What would her father have thought, if he could have seen her life's respectable conclusion? Would he have forgiven her at last? To that there was no answer. She drifted off again into dreams.

Janet Goldfinch

A Victorian Miss

Printed in Great Britain
by Amazon

81776669R00142